Somerset Dreams and Other Fictions

Somerset Dreams

AND OTHER FICTIONS

Kate Wilhelm

Foreword by R. Glenn Wright

PERENNIAL LIBRARY
Harper & Row, Publishers
New York, Hagerstown, San Francisco, London

Grateful acknowledgment is hereby made for permission to reprint the following:

"Somerset Dreams," first published in *Orbit 5*, copyright © 1969 by Damon Knight.

"The Encounter," first published in *Orbit 8*, copyright © 1970 by Damon Knight.

"Planet Story," first published in EPOCH, copyright © 1975 by Robert Silverberg and Roger Elwood.

"Symbiosis," first published in *Cosmopolitan*, copyright © 1972 The Hearst Corporation.

"Ladies and Gentlemen, This Is Your Crisis!," first published in *Orbit 18*, copyright © 1976 by Damon Knight.

"The Hounds," first published in *A SHOCKING THING*, copyright © 1974 by Damon Knight.

"State of Grace," first published in *Orbit 19*, copyright © 1977 by Damon Knight.

First PERENNIAL LIBRARY edition published 1979.

ISBN: 0-06-080476-9

79 80 81 82 83 10 9 8 7 6 5 4 3 2 1

Contents

Foreword by R. Glenn Wright   vii

Somerset Dreams   1

The Encounter   47

Planet Story   75

Mrs. Bagley Goes to Mars   91

Symbiosis   101

Ladies and Gentlemen, This Is Your Crisis   121

The Hounds   137

State of Grace   165

Foreword

The short story is one of those peripatetic forms of literature that, in its changing shape and form, is always threatening to get lost. But the public waits, watches, and still reads short stories because they satisfy the mind and emotions in a particular way. A good short story is like a well-cut precious stone—small, beautiful, faceted and faintly mysterious. Nothing else quite does what it can do. Kate Wilhelm is a superb practitioner of that special art, as this collection of her work so deftly illustrates.

One of Ms. Wilhelm's greatest gifts is her versatility. She is impossible to classify, and this characteristic is one of her greatest strengths. (It is also a reason why it is likely that not everyone will like all the stories in this book.) Of the eight stories in the present volume three could be labeled as science fiction: "Planet Story," "State of Grace" and "Mrs. Bagley Goes to Mars." Yet of the three probably only "Planet Story" is "hard core" science fiction. A team of men and women explore a planet full of abundant and complex life to ascertain if, in time, it should be colonized. The author makes clear that there is nothing to fear on the planet—the balance of nature is perfect and fitted for human life. But one after another of the explorers becomes subject to paralyzing fits of unreasoning, absolute terror. The planet is designated uninhabitable after four deaths, and no one ever understands quite why. This apparent Eden has no place for man, his fall or his glory. The story resonates with the fears of Adam and Cain.

Both "Mrs. Bagley Goes to Mars" and "State of Grace" are full of humor, a quality that is not ordinarily associated with Ms. Wilhelm's writing. In the former, Mrs. Bagley is the typical, bored, working mother of a teen-aged rotten kid. (Her work consists of sewing plastic covers for tanks or something.) Her husband does something in the Bronx. Joey the son is about to graduate, illiterate, from high school. Life is full of dreary desperation, so Mrs. Bagley goes to Mars, which isn't much different from earth. After a brief stay, and an even briefer return to her happy home, she leaves for good—for Ganymede.

"State of Grace" is also about a lower-middle-class couple, this time living in Florida, and minus the son. In their back yard is a huge oak tree, and in it are small, lemur-like creatures that may or may not actually exist. The wife is convinced that they do, and that they are magic, bringing good or bad luck according to treatment received. Howard, the husband, is half convinced that there is something special in the tree, and Wilhelm recounts his frustrated attempts to ferret out what the something is. He fails in various ludicrous fashions, and with no dignity whatsoever. It is his failure, and his wife's belief, that underscores the accuracy of the story's title.

Justly, Ms. Wilhelm is best known as a science fiction writer. The three stories briefly described above illustrate her skill with the genre. They also demonstrate a growing preoccupation of the author—the absurdity of so much of contemporary life. The angle of vision, that of satire not always gentle, is reminiscent of S. J. Perelman with more than a touch of Peter deVries. The writing is what may well be called social science fiction, which is the locus of at least half of the SF published today. Wilhelm seldom writes of man's involvement with the theories and hardware of modern chemistry, physics and technology. Instead, she carefully follows the technical "advances," and then, half by extrapolation and half by watching the newspapers, presents the reader with an unexpected (yet immediately recognizable) fusion of the two that illustrates the changed habits and lives of her characters—us.

"Ladies and Gentlemen, This Is Your Crisis" is her sharpest piece in this vein in the present volume. With absolutely no moral stated (Wilhelm never states morals, all is done by the indirection of absolute reality) she etches yet another design on the great abstract eye of our living rooms—television.

"Ladies and Gentlemen, This Is Your Crisis" is a study in counterpoint. A husband and wife of absolutely no redeeming social value whatsoever, and unpleasantly similar to the husband and wife of "Mrs. Bagley Goes to Mars" and "State of Grace," race home from work on a Friday afternoon to their very expensive wall television to watch the game show to end all game shows. The title of the program is the title of the story and involves four individuals (two men and two women) who are mentally ill. The way for them to get well is through Crisis Therapy, which involves the possibilities of sudden death, complete mental breakdown, and/or a prize of a million dollars, tax free. All or any of the above can and do take place live, on-camera. The program lasts, without break, from Friday noons to Sunday midnights and is horrible. Viewers, in this case the couple, Lottie and Butcher, live through the agonies of each of the "contestants" while living through their own pathetic passions that threaten mayhem and murder as the weekend proceeds. The story, aptly told through the cold eye of the third person, moves swiftly and is as devastating an indictment of the role of television in our contemporary social order as anything I have read.

Something striking has happened to Kate Wilhelm's writing over the last half-dozen years. Beginning somewhere around the time of her novel *Margaret and I* (1971), or perhaps even earlier with her novella *The Abyss* (1967), her vision has sharpened; her ability to tap the reader's unsuspecting unconscious has grown in strength and power; she is on the edge of being a major contemporary writer, and recognition of that fact is overdue.

I commented at the opening of this introduction that Ms. Wilhelm's writing was all but impossible to classify, and have then proceeded to talk of groups of stories with common themes or techniques. To my mind, if there is one element that is at the center of her strength as a writer, it is her ability to lift the edge off the surface of everyday reality—not to show us the seething incoherence of libido energy as so many contemporary authors do—rather, she lifts that edge to show us sometimes beautiful and always mysterious patterns underneath that we almost, but not quite, understand. We, all of us, desperately want and need to understand those patterns—they are fundamental somehow to our whole state of being, individually and as members of embattled Western culture. Wilhelm has sensed this need, she feels it, and at her best she helps us with those ever-so-strange patterns. Her stories make us stop stock-still, and, I guess the word is, listen.

Some analogies are in order. The best short stories of Katherine Ann Porter, "Pale Horse, Pale Rider," Daphne DuMaurier, "Kiss Me Again, Stranger," and Shirley Jackson, "The Lottery" all, in their own ways, have this same mysterious power; it appears unique to the short story form. It is also striking that the comparisons that came to mind are of works by twentieth century women. Just what the significance is I cannot say; I do not know, but I would like to.

There are three stories in this volume that illustrate this power. One is the title story, "Somerset Dreams"; the other two are "Symbiosis," and "The Hounds." I will leave "Symbiosis" to the readers' conjectures, but I would like to say something about the other two.

In some ways "Somerset Dreams" is more complex than "The Hounds." It is told in the first person, present tense; the effect is initially purposefully awkward and feeds into the story's im-

pact. It is about a young woman in her late twenties, Janet
Matthews, who is on summer vacation back in Somerset, the
small town she grew up in. Somerset is dying; there are only
forty old people left in it, all of whom Janet knows well. Almost
simultaneously with her arrival in the town, also arrive a Harvard professor of psychology and nine graduate students. They
have come to compare dream patterns of the urban-bred students with the inhabitants of Somerset. As one of the students
says,

> In the city we know pretty much what each of us dreams, we've
> been subjects and experimenters all year now, and we decided to
> hunt up a place where there were none of the same things at all and
> then run a comparison. . . . What we . . . expect is that our own
> dreams will change, but that the patterns of the dreams of the
> people already here will remain relatively stable.

The hypothesis is more than borne out. Janet, by profession
an anesthesiologist in New York City, agrees to help the Harvard team of researchers gain the cooperation of the local
townspeople in recording their dreams. The outcome of the
group's research, although logical, and consistent with much of
the contemporary work being done in dream research, is truly
horrifying.

"Somerset Dreams" is representative of Wilhelm's writing at
its best. The story is full of flashbacks, a technique that becomes
a part of the story's theme. And the theme itself, the multiple
means of slow, creeping death, is beautifully explored. A kaleidoscope of detail is given until the reader is enmeshed—
" . . . cul-de-sac. I say the word again and again to myself, liking
it very much, thinking what a wonderful word it is, so mysterious, so full of meanings, layers and layers of meanings." Or
again—"I can hear voices from the big room with its Victorian
furniture and the grandfather clock that always stutters on the
second tick. I hear it now: tick-t . . . t . . . tick." The connections
between dream research and the archetypal figure of the vam-

pire are only hinted at, that is enough. One also comes to appreciate the significance of Janet as anesthesiologist, one whose skill is to deliver "controlled, small doses of death." The kaleidoscope design becomes a three-dimensional maze, and slowly the horror of the situation fully ensnares the reader. Hallucination, dream and memory make up the three dimensions of the story's maze, and the Minotaur in the middle of the maze is the death wish we all recognize. He is an unfortunately beautiful animal.

The heroine of "Somerset Dreams" at one place in the story says of the students studying the town—"I think of them as so very young, prying into things they cannot understand, trying to find answers that, if found, will make them question all of reality." Wilhelm's art can do that very thing, make us question the nature of reality, and that, indeed, is her aim. Her fiction pries, probes, suggests meanings that her readers respond to in ways almost primitive. The process is often not very pleasant: there is a touch of the Greek in her, both Plato and Euripides. Enlightenment is there, but not without its perils.

In conversation once I asked her about "The Hounds," to me the most forceful story in the collection. It is a longish story and limns out clearly what I have been seeking to describe in her short fiction. She said, and I believe her, that she was puzzled by the story, that she didn't really understand it or why she wrote it. There are undoubtedly many ways to interpret "The Hounds." To me it is a fable—a chilling reworking of the Greek myth of the goddess Artemis (or Diana) and the hunter Actaeon. The original myth is starkly simple. Diana, goddess of the moon and of the hunt, was notoriously chaste. She would have nothing to do with males, either mortal or divine. She lived in the forest and was both very private and very jealous. Actaeon was the classic Greek youth of skill and beauty, and a devotee of the goddess. One day, while hunting, he accidentally stumbled upon the goddess at her bath. Except under extraordinary circumstances no mortal could look upon a god and live. Though the circumstances were accidental and extraordinary in retrospect, Diana's punishment of the unsuspecting youth was sure and swift: she changed the man into a stag and he was torn to pieces by his own hunting dogs.

"The Hounds" is the story of Rose Ellen and her husband Martin. Like many of the scientists involved with the space program in Florida a few years back, at forty-nine Martin loses his position when the government money runs out. Deciding not to look for another job in his field he opts instead to return to the land and buys a small farm in Kentucky.

Rose Ellen is opposed to this (it turns out that she has grown up on a small farm with a father who drank and was killed—while drunk—in a head-on car accident), but she has always played the role of the dutiful wife, quiet, loving, but intelligently submissive. The move from affluent, suburban Florida to rural Kentucky is accomplished with so little trauma that everyone is surprised. The three children adjust with ease; Martin gets a job in the local high school teaching general science and Rose Ellen does substitute teaching in the grade school. All is placid.

Enter the dogs, two of them, probably salukis. They are incredibly beautiful—lean, sleek, with soft flowing silver hair and great golden eyes. They follow Rose Ellen home from school one day and are hers, attaching themselves to her with completely unmenacing possession. From the outset Rose is unreasoningly terrified of them.

I will not describe the remainder of the story, but only mention some details that are significant. When Rose Ellen first remembers her father, just before she sees the dogs for the first time, it is a memory of how he used to fight with her mother —violent arguments that ended in reconciliations in bed. "They fought like animals." Rose Ellen and Martin never fight; not, at any rate, until after the arrival of the hounds.

Her father had a hunting dog, a hound, that her mother let loose one day. It never came back, but one could hear its distinctive howl in the night.

Rose Ellen will not, cannot, touch the dogs. When Martin

does, the first time, his reaction is extremely sensual, almost sexual. But Rose's recurring dream makes it clear that if she ever petted them, embraced them, she would be trapped forever; they would never let her go. It is the dream itself that is the key to the story. There she is, the woman in white, riding with the hounds to the hunt. Their prey is a stag, and should she dream the dream once more, she, knife in hand, would be involved in the kill itself; her marriage would end and her life be destroyed.

The story finally is about freedom, or rather, about license, the necessary license that is associated with the god of wine and drunkenness, Dionysus. Rose Ellen has never fully experienced this abandon. It is associated with her father and death and the dogs. A part of her wants it—to be Diana, to be one with nature, to be Mother Nature's archetypal feminine destroyer. But it cannot be, not for Rose Ellen, or for most of us in this civilized last quarter of the twentieth century. Our power over (with?) Nature is too great. There is too much at stake.

So these are some of the things Kate Wilhelm writes about. She is very gifted, and she tells us both more and less about the world we live in, and about tomorrow, than we may wish to know. Read with pleasure. Here is an artist at work.

R. GLENN WRIGHT

East Lansing, Michigan
September, 1977

Somerset Dreams and Other Fictions

Somerset Dreams

I AM ALONE in my mother's house, listening to the ghosts who live here now, studying the shadowed features of the moon that is incredibly white in a milky sky. It is easier to believe that it is a face lined with care than to accept mountains and craters. There a nose, long and beaked, there a mouth, dark, partially open. A broad creased forehead . . . They say that children believe the sun and moon follow them about. Not only children . . . Why just a face? Where is the rest of the body? Submerged in an ethereal fluid that deceives one into believing it does not exist? Only when this captive body comes into view, stirring the waters, clouding them, does one realize that space is not empty at all. When the moon passes, and the sky clears once more, the other lights are still there. Other faces at incredible distances? I wonder what the bodies of such brilliant swimmers must be like. But I turn my gaze from the moon, feeling now the hypnotic spell, wrenching free of it.

The yard has turned silvery and lovely although it is not a lovely place any more. Below the rustlings in the house I hear the water of Cobb's Run rippling softly, breaking on the remains of an old dam. It will be cool by the flowing water, I think, and I pull on shorts and a blouse. I wonder how many others are out in the moonlight. I know there are some. Does anyone sleep peacefully in Somerset now? I would like to wander out by the brook with nothing on, but even to think of it makes me smile. Someone would see me, and by morning there would be stories of a young naked woman, and by noon the naked woman would be a ghost pointing here and there. By evening old Mr. Larson, or Miss Louise, would be dead. Each is waiting only for the sign that it is time.

I anoint myself with insect repellent. It is guaranteed to be odorless, but I can smell it anyway, and can feel it, greaseless and very wet, on my arms and legs.

I slip from the house where my mother and father are sleeping. The night is still hot, our house doesn't cool off until almost morning, and there is no wind at all, only the moon that fills the sky. Someone is giggling in the yard and I shush her, too close to the house, to Mother's windows on the second floor. We race down the path to the pool made by damming the run and we jump into the silver-sheened water. Someone grabs my ankle and I hold my breath and wrestle under the surface with one of the boys. I can't tell which one it is. Now and then someone lets a shriek escape and we are motionless, afraid Father will appear and order us out. We play in the water at least an hour, until the wind starts and blows the mosquitoes away, and then we stumble over the rocks and out to the grass where now the night is cool and we are pleasantly tired and ready for sleep. When I get back to the house I see the door closing and I stop, holding my breath. I listen as hard as I can, and finally hear the tread on the steps: Father, going back to bed.

I slip on sandals and pick up my cigarettes and lighter without turning on the light. The moonlight is enough. In the hall I pause outside the door of my parents' room, and then go down the stairs. I don't need a light in this house, even after a year's absence. The whole downstairs is wide open, the kitchen door, the front door, all the windows. Only the screens are between me and the world. I think of the barred windows of my 87th

Street apartment and smile again, and think how good to be free and home once more. The night air is still and warm, perfumed with grass and phlox and the rambling rose on the garage trellis. I had forgotten how much stronger the fragrance is at night. The mosquitoes are whining about my face, but they don't land on me. The path has grown up now with weeds and volunteer columbines and snapdragons. By day it is an unruly strip with splashes of brilliant colors, now it is silver and gray and dark red.

At the creek I find a smooth rock and sit on it, not thinking, watching the light change on the moving water, and when the wind starts to blow, I think it must be three in the morning. I return to the unquiet house and go to bed, and this time I am able to fall asleep.

I walk to town, remembering how I used to skip, or ride my bike on the sidewalks that were large limestone slabs, as slick as polished marble when they were wet. I am bemused by the tilted slabs, thinking of the ground below shoving and trying to rid itself of their weight. I am more bemused by myself; I detest people who assign anthropomorphic concepts to nature. I don't do it anywhere but here in Somerset. I wear a shift to town, observing the customs even now. After high school, girls no longer wore shorts, or pants, in town.

I have been counting: seven closed-up houses on First Street. Our house is at the far end of First Street, one ninth of a mile from the other end of town where Magnolia Avenue starts up the mountain as Highway 590. All the side streets are named for flowers. I pass Wisteria Avenue and see that the wicker furniture is still on the porch of Sagamore House. The apple trees are still there, gnarled, like the hands of men so old that they are curling in on themselves, no longer able to reach for the world, no longer desiring the world. I come back every year, and every year I am surprised to see that some things are unchanged. The four apple trees in the yard of the Sagamore House are important to me; I am always afraid that this year they will have been cut down or felled by one of the tornadoes that now and again roar like express trains from the southwest, to die in the mountains beyond the town.

How matter-of-factly we accepted the long, hot, dry summers, the soul-killing winters, the droughts, the tornadoes, the blizzards. The worst weather in any part of the country is equaled in Somerset. We accept it as normal.

I am not certain why the apple trees are so important. In the early spring, tempted by a hot sun into folly, they bloom prematurely year after year, and are like torches of white light. There is always a late frost that turns them black, and then they are just trees, growing more and more crooked, producing scant fruit, lovely to climb, however.

In Mr. Larson's store, where I buy my groceries when I am home, I learn from Agnes McCombs that a station wagon and two cars have arrived early this morning with students and a doctor from Harvard. Agnes leaves and I say goodbye absently. I am thinking of yet another rite of passage that took place here, in old Mr. Larson's store when I was thirteen. He always handed out chunks of "homemade baloney" to the children while their mothers shopped, but that day, with the tidbit extended, he regarded me with twinkling eyes and withdrew the meat impaled on a two-pronged fork. "Mebbe you'd like a Coke, Miss Janet?"

He is so old, eighty, ninety. I used to think he was a hundred then, and he changes little. His hands are like the apple trees. I ask him, "Why are they here? What are they doing?"

"Didn't say. Good to see you home again, Janet. The old house need any repairs?"

"Everything's fine. Why'd Miss Dorothea let them in?"

"Money. Been six, seven years since anyone's put up at the Sagamore. Taxes don't go down much, you know."

I can't explain the fury that is threatening to explode within me, erupting to the surface as tears, or a fishwife's scolding. Mr. Larson nods. "We figured that mebbe you could sidle up to 'em.

Find out what they're up to." He rummages under the counter and brings out a letter. "From your dad," he says, peering at the return address. "He still thriving?"

"About the same. I visited him last month. I guess he thought of things he forgot to tell me and put them in a letter."

Mr. Larson shakes his head sadly. "A fine man, your dad." After a moment, he adds, "Could be for the best, I reckon."

I know what he means, that without Mother, with the town like it is, with his only child a woman nearing thirty . . . But he doesn't know what Father is like or he couldn't say that. I finish my shopping and greet Poor Haddie, who is back with the truck. He's been making his delivery to the Sagamore House. He will bring my things later. Leaving, I try to say to myself Haddie without the Poor and the word sounds naked, the name of a stranger, not of the lumbering delivery "boy" I have known all my life.

I have other visits to make. Dr. Warren's shingle needs a bit of paint, I note as I enter his house. He doesn't really practice now, although people talk to him about their sore throats and their aches and pains, and now and again he suggests that this or that might help. If they get really ill, they go to Hawley, twenty-eight miles away, over the mountain. Dr. Warren never fails to warn me that the world isn't ready for a lady doctor, and I still try to tell him that I am probably one of the highest-paid anesthesiologists in the world, but he forgets in the intervening year. I always end up listening to advice about sticking with nursing where a woman is really accepted. Dr. Warren delivered me back there at the house in the upstairs bedroom, with my father assisting gravely, although later he broke down and cried like a baby himself, or so Dr. Warren said. I suspect he did.

Dr. Warren and his wife, Norma, make a fuss over me and tears are standing in my eyes as they serve me coffee with cream so thick that it has to be scooped up in a spoon. They too seem to think I will find out what the flatland foreigners want with our town.

Sagamore House. I try to see it again with the eyes of my childhood: romantic, forbidding, magnificent, with heavy drapes and massive, ornately carved furniture. I have a snapshot memory of crawling among the clawed feet, staring eye to eye at the lions and gargoyles and sticking out my tongue at them. The hotel has shrunk, the magic paled and the castle become merely a three-storied wooden building, with cupolas and many chimneys and gables, gray, like everything else in the town. Only the apple trees on the wide velvety lawn are still magic. I enter by the back door and surprise Miss Dorothea and Miss Annie, who are bustling about with an air of frantic haste.

There are cries and real tears and many pats and kisses, and the inevitable coffee, and then I am seated at the long work table with a colander of unshelled peas in my lap, and a pan for them.

". . . and they said it wasn't possible to send the bus any more. Not twenty-eight miles each way twice a day. And you can't argue with that since no one's done a thing about the road in four years and it's getting so dangerous that . . ."

A cul-de-sac, I am thinking, listening first to Dorothea and then to Annie, and sometimes both together. Somerset used to be the link between Hawley and Jefferson, but a dam was built on the river and the bridge was inundated, and now Somerset lies dying in a cul-de-sac. I say the word again and again to myself, liking it very much, thinking what a wonderful word it is, so mysterious, so full of meanings, layers and layers of meanings. . . .

I know they want to hear about my father, but won't ask, so I tell them that I saw him last month and that he is about the same. And the subject changes briskly, back to the departure of the last four families with school-age children.

The door from the lobby is pushed open and the Harvard doctor steps inside the kitchen. I don't like him. I can't decide if it is actually hatred, or simple dislike, but I wish he were not here, that he had stayed at Harvard. He is fortyish, pink and paunchy, with soft pink hands, and thin brown hair. I suspect that he whines when he doesn't get his way.

"Miss Dorothea, I wonder if you can tell me where the boys can rent a boat, and buy fishing things?" It registers on him that he doesn't know me and he stares pointedly.

I say, "I'm Janet Matthews."

"Oh, do you live here, too?"

Manners of a pig, I think, and I nod. "At the end of First Street. The big white house that's afloat in a sea of weeds."

He has trouble fitting me into his list of characters. He introduces himself after a long pause while he puckers his forehead and purses his lips. I am proud of Dorothea and Annie for leaving him alone to flounder. I know it is an effort for them. He says, "I am Dr. Staunton."

"Medical doctor."

"No." He starts to turn back toward the door and I stop him again.

"What is your doctorate, Dr. Staunton?"

I can almost hear the gasp from Dorothea, although no sound issues.

"Psychology," he says, and clearly he is in a bad temper now. He doesn't wait for any more questions, or the answer to his question to Dorothea.

I go back to shelling the peas and Annie rolls out her piecrust and Dorothea turns her attention back to the Newburg sauce that she hasn't stopped stirring once. A giggle comes from Annie, and we all ignore it. Presently the peas are finished and I leave to continue my walk through the town, gradually making my way home, stopping to visit several other people on the way. Decay and death are spreading in Somerset, like a disease that starts very slowly, in a hidden place, and emerges only when it is assured of absolute success in the destruction of the host.

The afternoon is very hot and still, and I try to sleep, but give it up after fifteen minutes. I think of the canoe that we used to keep in the garage, and I think of the lake that is a mile away, and presently I am wrestling with the car carriers, and then getting the canoe hoisted up, scratching the finish on the car.

I float down the river in silence, surprising a beaver and three or four frolicking otters; I see a covey of quail rise with an absurd noise like a herd of horses. A fish jumps, almost landing in the canoe. I have sneaked out alone, determined this time to take the rapids, with no audience, no one to applaud my success, or to stand in fearful silence and watch me fail. The current becomes swifter and I can hear the muted roar, still far ahead, but it seems that any chances to change my mind are flashing by too fast to be seized now, and I know that I am afraid, terribly afraid of the white water and the rocks and sharp pitches and deceptive pools that suck and suck in a never-ending circle of death. I want to shoot the rapids, and I am so afraid. The roar grows and it is all there is, and now the current is an express belt, carrying me along on its surface with no side eddies or curves. It goes straight to the rocks. I can't turn the canoe. At the last minute I jump out and swim desperately away from the band of swift water, and I am crying and blinded by my tears and I find my way to shore by the feel of the current. I scrape my knees on a rock and stand up and walk from the river to fall face down in the weeds that line the banks. The canoe is lost, and I won't tell anyone what has happened. The following summer he buys another canoe, but I never try the rapids again.

And now there are no more rapids. Only a placid lake with muddy shores and thick water at this end, dark with algae and water hyacinths. I am so hot after getting the canoe on the car, and the air is so heavy that it feels ominous. A storm will come up, I decide. It excites me and I know that I want to be at home when the wind blows. I want to watch the ash tree in the wind, and following the thought, I realize that I want to see the ash tree blown down. This shocks me. It is so childish. Have I ever admitted to anyone, to myself even, why I come back each summer? I can't help myself. I am fascinated by death, I suppose. Daily at the hospital I administer death in small doses, controlled death, temporary death. I am compelled to come home because here too is death. It is like being drawn to the bedside of a loved one that you know is dying, and being at once awed and frightened, and curious about what death is like ultimately. We try so hard to hide the curiosity from the others, the strangers. And that is why I hate the Harvard doctor so much: he is intruding in a family matter. This is our death, not his, to watch and to weep over and mourn. I know that somehow he has learned of this death and it is that which has drawn him, just as it draws me, and I refuse him the right to partake of our sorrow, to test our grief, to measure our loss.

The storm hangs over the horizon out of sight. The change in air pressure depresses me, and the sullen heat, and the unkempt yard, and the empty house that nevertheless rustles with unseen life. Finally I take the letter from Father from my pocket and open it. I don't weep over his letters any longer, but the memory of the paroxysms of the past fills me with the aftertaste of tears as I stare at the childish scrawl: large, ungraceful letters, carefully traced and shaky, formed with too much pressure so that the paper is pierced here and there, the back of the sheet like Braille.

It is brief and inane, as I have known it would be; a cry for release from Them, a prayer to an unhearing child who has become a god, or at least a parent, for forgiveness. Statistics: every year fifty thousand are killed, and she was one of them, and 1.9 million are disabled, and he was one of them. Do all the disabled bear this load of guilt that consumes him daily? He is Prometheus, his bed the rock, his guilt the devouring eagles. The gods wear white coats, and carry magic wands with which they renew him nightly so that he may die by day.

Why doesn't the storm come?

I wait for the storm and don't go down to the lake after all. Another day, I tell myself, and leave the canoe on the car top.

I mix a gin and tonic and wander with it to the back yard where nothing moves now. I stare up at the ash tree; it has grown so high and straight in the twenty years since we planted it. I remember the lightning that shredded the cherry tree that once stood there, the splinters of white wood that I picked up all over the yard afterward. The following week Father brought home the tiny ash stick and very solemnly we planted it in the same spot. I cried because it wasn't another cherry tree. I smile, recalling my tears and the tantrum, and the near ritual of the tree planting. At eight I was too old for the tears and the tantrum, but neither Father nor Mother objected. I sit in the yard, letting the past glide in and out of my mind without trying to stop the flow.

At six I dress for dinner with Dr. Warren and Norma. This is our new ritual. My first evening home I dine with the doctor and his wife. They are very lonely, I suspect, although neither says so. I walk through the quiet town as it dozes in the evening, the few occupied houses tightly shaded and closed against the heat. Norma had air-conditioning installed years ago and her house chills me when I first enter. She ushers me to the far side, to a glassed porch that is walled with vines and coleus plants with yellow, red, white leaves, and a funny little fountain that has blue-tinted water splashing over large enameled clam shells. I hesitate at the doorway to the porch. Dr. Staunton is there, holding a glass of Norma's special summer drink which contains lime juice, rum, honey, soda water, and God knows what else. He is speaking very earnestly to Dr. Warren, and both rise when they see me.

"Miss Matthews, how nice to see you again." Dr. Staunton bows slightly, and Dr. Warren pulls a wicker chair closer to his own for me. He hands me a glass.

"Edgar has been telling me about the research he's doing up here with the boys," Dr. Warren says.

Edgar? I nod, and sip the drink.

"I really was asking Blair for his assistance," Edgar Staunton says, smiling, but not on the inside. I wonder if he ever smiles on the inside.

Blair. I glance at Dr. Warren, who will forever be Dr. Warren to me, and wonder at the easy familiarity. Has he been so lonesome that he succumbed to the first outsider who came in and treated him like a doctor and asked for help?

"What is your research, Dr. Staunton?" I ask.

He doesn't tell me to use his first name. He says, "I brought some of my graduate students who are interested in the study of dreams, and we are using your town as a more or less controlled environment. I was wondering if some of the local people might like to participate, also."

Vampire, I thought. Sleeping by day, manning the electroencephalograph by night, guarding the electrodes, reading the pen tracings, sucking out the inner life of the volunteers, feeding on the wishes and fears . . .

"How exactly does one go about doing dream research?" I ask.

"What we would like from your townspeople is a simple record of the dreams they recall on awakening. Before they even get up, or stir much at all, we'd like for them to jot down what they remember of the dreams they've had during the night. We don't want them to sign them, or indicate in any way whose dreams they are, you understand. We aren't trying to analyze anyone, just sample the dreams."

I nod, and turn my attention to the splashing water in the fountain. "I thought they used machines, or something. . . ."

I can hear the slight edge in his voice again as he says, "On the student volunteers only, or others who volunteer for that kind of experimentation. Would you be interested in participating, Miss Matthews?"

"I don't know. I might be. Just what do you mean by controlled environment?"

"The stimuli are extremely limited by the conditions of the town, its lack of sensory variety, the absence of television or

movies, its isolation from any of the influences of a metropolitan
cultural center. The stimuli presented to the volunteers will be
almost exactly the same as those experienced by the inhabitants
of the town. . . ."

"Why, Dr. Staunton, we have television here, and there are
movie houses in Hawley, and even summer concerts." Norma
stands in the doorway holding a tray of thumbnail-sized biscuits
filled with savory sausage, and her blue eyes snap indignantly
as she turns from the psychologist to her husband, who is quietly
regarding the Harvard doctor.

"Yes, but I understand that the reception is very poor and you
are limited to two channels, which few bother to watch."

"When there's something on worthwhile to watch, we tune
in, but we haven't allowed ourselves to become addicted to it,"
Norma says.

I wish Norma could have waited another minute or two before stopping him, but there will be time, through dinner, after
dinner. We will return to his research. I take one of the pastries
and watch Staunton and Dr. Warren, and listen to the talk that
has now turned to the value of the dam on the river, and the
growth in tourism at the far end of the valley, and the stagna-
tion at this end. Staunton knows about it all. I wonder if he has
had a computer search out just the right spot for his studies, find
just the right-sized town, with the correct number of people,
and the appropriate kind of eliciting stimuli. There are only
twenty-two families in the town now, a total population of forty-
one, counting me. Probably he can get five or six of them to help
him, and with eight students, that would be a fair simple. For
what, I don't know.

I listen again to the Harvard doctor. "I wasn't certain that
your townspeople would even speak to us, from what I'd heard
about the suspicions of rural villages and the like."

"How ridiculous," Norma says.

"Yes, so I am learning. I must say the reception we have
received has heartened me tremendously."

I smile into my drink, and I know that he will find everyone very friendly, ready to say good morning, good afternoon, how're things, nice weather. Wait until he tries to draw them into reporting dreams, I tell myself. I know Dr. Warren is thinking this too, but neither of us says anything.

"I would like your help in particular, Blair," Edgar says, smiling very openly now. "And yours, Norma." I swallow some of the ice and watch Norma over the rim of the glass. She is terribly polite now, with such a sweet smile on her pretty face, and her eyes so calm and friendly.

"Really, Dr. Staunton? I can't imagine why. I mean, I never seem to recall anything I dream no matter how hard I try." Norma realizes that the tray is not being passed around, and she picks it up and invites Staunton to help himself.

"That's the beauty of this project," Staunton says, holding one of the tiny biscuits almost to his lips. "Most people say the same thing, and then they find out that they really do dream, quite a lot in fact, and that if they try to remember before they get out of bed, why, they can recapture most of it." He pops the biscuit into his mouth and touches his fingertips to the napkin spread on his knees.

"But, Dr. Staunton, I don't dream," Norma says, even more friendly than before, urging another of the biscuits on him, smiling at him. He really shouldn't have called her Norma.

"But everybody dreams. . . ."

"Oh, is that what your books teach? How strange of them." Norma notices that our glasses are almost empty, and excuses herself, to return in a moment with the pitcher.

Dr. Warren has said nothing during the exchange between Norma and Staunton. I can see the crinkle lines that come and go about his eyes, but that is because I know where to look. He remains very serious when Staunton turns to him.

"You would be willing to cooperate, wouldn't you, Blair? I mean, you understand the necessity of this sort of research."

"Yes, of course, except that I'm a real ogre when I wake up.

Takes an hour, two hours for me to get charged up for the day. My metabolism is so low in the hours just before and after dawn, I'm certain that I would be a washout for your purposes, and by the time I'm human again, the night has become as if it never existed for me."

Dr. Staunton is not sipping any longer. He takes a long swallow and then another. He is not scowling, but I feel that if he doesn't let it show, he will have an attack of ulcers, or at least indigestion, before the night is over. He has no more liking for me than I have for him, but he forces the smile back into place and it is my turn.

"Miss Matthews?"

"I haven't decided yet," I say. "I'm curious about it, and I do dream. I read an article somewhere, in *Time*, or *Newsweek*, or someplace, and it sounds very mysterious, but I don't like the idea of the wires in the brain, and the earphones and all."

Very patiently he explains again that only his student volunteers use the equipment, and others who specifically volunteer for that phase. I ask if I might see how they use it sometime, and he is forced to say yes. He tries to get my yes in return, but I am coy and say only that I have to think about it first. He tries to get Dr. Warren to promise to approach other people in the town, try to get their cooperation for him, and Dr. Warren sidesteps adroitly. I know the thought will occur to him to use me for that purpose, but it doesn't that evening. I decide that he isn't terribly bright. I wonder about his students, and I invite him to bring them, all of them, to my house for an outdoor barbecue the following night. That is all he gets from any of us, and dinner seems very slow, although, as usual, very good. Staunton excuses himself quickly after dinner, saying, with his off-again, on-again smile, that he must return to work, that only the fortunate are allowed their nights of rest.

No one argues with him, or urges him to linger, and when he is gone I help Norma with the dishes and Dr. Warren sits in the kitchen having black coffee, and we talk about the Harvard doctor.

"I plain don't like him," Norma says with conviction. "Slimy man."

I think of his pink face and pink hairless hands, and his cheeks that shake when he walks, and I know what she means.

"I guess his project isn't altogether bad, or a complete waste of time," Dr. Warren says. "Just got the wrong place, wrong time, wrong people."

"I want to find out exactly what he expects to prove," I say. "I wonder what sort of contrast he expects between students and our people. That might even be interesting." I wonder if the research is really his, or the idea of one of his graduate students. I try not to draw conclusions yet. I can wait until the next night when I'll meet them all. I say, "Dr. Warren, Father keeps begging me to bring him home. Do you think it would help him?"

Dr. Warren puts down his cup and studies me hard. "Bedridden still?"

"Yes, and always will be, but I could manage him in the dining room downstairs. He's so unhappy in the nursing home. I'm sure the house, the noises there would bring back other days to him, make him more cheerful."

"It's been four years now, hasn't it?" Dr. Warren knows that. I wonder why he is playing for time, what thoughts he has that he doesn't want to express. "Honey," he says, in the gentle voice that used to go with the announcement of the need for a needle, or a few stitches. I remember that he never promised that it wouldn't hurt if it would. "I think you'd be making a mistake. Is he really unhappy? Or does he just have moments when he wants the past given back to him?"

I feel angry with him suddenly for not understanding that when Father is lucid he wants to be home. I can only shrug.

"Think on it, Janet. Just don't decide too fast." His face is old suddenly, and I realize that everyone in Somerset is aged. It's like walking among the pyramids, at a distance forever changeless, but on closer inspection constant reminders of aging, of senescence, of usefulness past and nearly forgotten. I turn to stare at Norma and see her as she is, not as she was when I was a child waiting for a cookie fresh and still warm, with the middle soft and the top crackly with sugar. I feel bewildered by both of them, outraged that they should reveal themselves so to me. There is a nearby crack of thunder, sharp-edged and explosive, not the rolling kind that starts and ends with an echo of itself, but a rifle blast. I stare out the window at lightning, jagged and brilliant, as sharply delineated as the thunder.

"I should go before the downpour," I say.

"I'll drive you," Dr. Warren says, but I won't let him.

"I'll make it before the rain. Maybe it's cooler now."

Inconsequentials that fill the days and nights of our lives, nonsequiturs that pass for conversation and thought, pleasantries, promises, we rattle them off comfortingly and I am walking down the street toward my house, not on the sidewalk, but in the street, where walking is easier.

The wind starts to blow when I am halfway between Magnolia and Rose Streets. I can see the Sagamore House ahead and I decide to stop there and wait for the rain to come and go. Probably I have planned this in a dark corner of my mind, but I have not consciously decided to visit the students so soon. I hurry, and the wind now has the town astir, filled with the same rustles that fill my house; scurrying ghosts, what have they to worry about if the rain should come before they settle in for the night?

Along First Street most of the buildings are closed forever. The ten-cent store, a diner, fabric shop, all sharing a common front, all locked, with large soaped loops linking the wide windows one to one. The rain starts, enormous drops that are wind-driven and hard. I can hear them against the tin roof of Mr. Larson's store and they sound like hailstones, but then the wind drowns all noise but its own. Thunder and lightning now, and the mad wind. I run the rest of the way to Sagamore House and arrive there almost dry, but completely breathless.

"Honey, for heaven's sake, come in and get some coffee!"

Dorothea starts to lead me to the kitchen, but I shake my head and incline it toward the parlor off to the left of the entrance.

"I'll go in there and wait out the storm, if you don't mind." I can hear voices from the big room with its Victorian furniture and the grandfather clock that always stutters on the second tick. I hear it now: tick—t . . . t . . . tick.

"I'll bring you a pot of coffee there, Janet," Dorothea says with a nod. When she comes back with the tray and the china cup and the silver pot, she will call me Miss Matthews.

I try to pat my hair down as I go into the parlor, and I know that I still present a picture of a girl caught in a sudden storm. I brush my arms, as if they are still wet, although they are not, and I shake my head, and at that moment there is another very close, very loud thunder crash, as if to justify my action. The boys stop talking when I enter. They are what I have known most of my life since college: young, fresh-looking, indistinguishable from seniors and graduate students the world over.

I smile generally at them and sit down on one of the red velour couches with a coffee table before it that has a bowl of white roses, a dish of peppermints, magazines, three ashtrays, each carved and enameled and spotless. The whole room is like that: chairs and chairs, all carved, waxed, gleaming, footstools, end tables, console tables, Tiffany lampshades on cut-glass lamps . . . The boys are at the other end of the room, six of them, two on the floor, the others in chairs, smoking, sipping beer or tall drinks. Dr. Staunton isn't there.

Dorothea brings my tray and does call me Miss Matthews and asks if I'd like anything else. I shake my head and she leaves me alone with the boys. There is a whispered conversation at the other end of the room, and one of the boys rises and comes to stand near me.

"Hi, I'm Roger Philpott. Are you Janet Matthews? I think you invited us all to dinner at your house tomorrow." Tall, thin, blond, very young-looking.

I grin back and nod. I look toward the others and say, "Maybe

by meeting just a few of you now, I'll be able to keep your
names straight."

Roger introduces the others, and I remember that there is a
Johnny, a Victor, Doug, Sid, and Mickey. No one is grotesque,
or even memorable. They regroup around me. Outside we can
hear the hail, undeniably hail now, and the wind shrieking in
the gables and eaves, all dwarfed by the intermittent explosions
of the thunder. Several times the lights flicker, and Dorothea
returns with hurricane lamps that she places in strategic places,
after a glance to see if I have accomplished my goal of becoming
part of the group of students.

Roger switches to coffee, but the other students reorder beer
and gin and bitter lemon, and Dorothea leaves us again. Roger
says, "I don't know how long some of us will be able to take life
in the country. What do you do around here?"

I laugh and say, "I come here to rest each summer. I live in
New York the rest of the year."

His interest quickens. "Oh, you work in the city then?"

"Yes, Columbia Medical Center. I'm an anesthesiologist."

"Dr. Staunton didn't mention that. He seems to think that all
the people here are locals."

"I didn't tell him," I say. He nods and I know that he realizes
that I have played the part of a local yokel with his superior. I
ask, "Is this his research, or is it the thesis of one of the boys?"

One of the others laughs. "It's Roger's original idea," he says.
"And mine." I try to remember which one he is and I think he
is Sid. Mediterranean type. I glance over the other faces, and
none shows surprise. So Staunton has taken over openly, and
they accept it as natural. It tells me more than they can know
about Staunton.

"You see, I had this idea that the whole pattern of dream
content might switch depending on the location of the
dreamer. In the city we know pretty much what each of us
dreams, we've been subjects and experimenters all year now,
and we decided to hunt up a place where there were none of

the same things at all and then run a comparison."

"And you'll check that against what you can find out from the people here, to see if there's a correlation?"

"We don't expect one," Sid said. "What we do expect is that our own dreams will change, but that the patterns of the dreams of the people already here will remain relatively stable."

"And what do you expect to prove?"

"I don't know that we'll prove anything, but assuming that dreams reflect the emotional states of the person, by examining them in varying circumstances we might get a clue about how to help people relax more than they do, what kind of vacation to plan for, how long to stay, things like that. If my reasoning is right, then we'll be able to predict from personality sketches whether a three-week vacation is desirable, or shorter periods more frequently. You see?"

I nod and can find no fault with the experiment. It does seem a legitimate line of research, and a useful one, perhaps. "I suppose you will have a computer run the analysis of dream content?"

Sid nods, and Roger says, "Would you like to see one of the cards we fill out? We've broken down dream content into categories. Like sexual with subheadings of hetero, homo, socially accepted, socially unaccepted, and so on, and a further breakdown of overt, covert; participatory, observed; satisfying, frustrating, and so on. I think we've hit everything."

"I would like to see one," I say, and he nods.

"I'll bring one out to your place with us tomorrow. Have you seen any of the sleep lab equipment?"

"Not in this context, not used in these experiments."

"Great. The first afternoon, after three or four, that you can get up here, I'll show you around."

"Perhaps tomorrow?" I say. "Will Dr. Staunton object?"

Roger and Sid exchange a hurried glance and Roger shrugs. "It's my research," he says.

"Is he setting up equipment, testing it out now?"

"No. In fact, he came home with indigestion, I think, and conked out right away."

I can't still the sudden laugh that I feel. I finish my coffee and stand up. "The storm is over, I think. At least it's catching its breath now. I'm glad I was forced to stop," I say, and hold out my hand to Roger and then Sid. "I must say, however, that I'm afraid Somerset isn't quite what you expected. I hope you won't be too disappointed in us."

"Will you help?" Roger asks.

I hesitate and then nod. "I used to keep a record for my own psychology classes. I'll start again."

"Thanks."

"If anyone in town asks my opinion," I say, standing in the open doorway now, feeling the cool wind that the storm has brought in, "I'll tell them that I'm cooperating, nothing more. They may or may not pay any attention to what I say."

"See you tomorrow afternoon," Roger says and I leave them and walk home. It is very dark now, and the rain smells fresh, the air is cool and clean. I am thinking of the two halves that make up the whole me. In the city I am brisk and efficient. I know the nurses talk about me, wondering if I am a lesbian (I'm not), if I have any sex life at all (not now). They are afraid of me because I will not permit any sloppiness in surgery, and I am quick to report them. They don't understand that my instruments are to me what the surgeon's scalpel is to him, and they think I worship dials and stainless-steel gods. I once heard myself described as more machine-like than any of the exotic equipment that I have mastered. I know that the thought of those boys staring at the charts of their alpha and beta rhythms has brought this retrospective mood but I can't break out of it. I continue to inspect my life as if from the outside. What no one understands is that it is not the machines that are deified, but the processes that the machines record, the fluctuations and the rhythms, the cyclic patterns that are beautiful when they are normal, and as hideous as a physical deformity when they are wrong. The covered mound on the hard table is meaningless when I observe it. Less than human, inert, it might be a corpse already, or a covered log, or a cache of potatoes. But the dials that I read tell me all I can know about it: male, steady heart, respiration normal . . . Body processes that add up to life, or non-life. What more is there?

My house is cool now, and rain has blown in the kitchen and dining-room windows. I mop it up and wipe the sills carefully, and inspect the rest of the house. I can't see anything in the yard, but I stand on the back porch and feel the coolness and the mistiness of the air until I start to shiver.

I have read that dreams follow a pattern of their own. The first dreams of the night are of events nearby in time and space, and as sleep progresses and the night goes by the dreams wander farther afield, into the past, or into future fantasy, and toward morning, they return to the here and now of the dreamer. During the night I wake up three times and jot down the dreams I can recall.

Dream number one is a simple-minded wish fulfillment. I am at a party where I sparkle and dazzle everyone in the house. It is an unfamiliar house, not unlike the Sagamore House, except more elegant, simpler, with cool white marble statues replacing the clutter. I am the belle of the party and I dance with everyone there, and in the center of the room is a champagne glass that must hold gallons. Looking through the bubbling wine, I see the statues shimmer and appear to come alive, but I know that it is only because of the rising bubbles, that it is an illusion. I am swept back to the dance floor and I swirl around in a delirium of joy.

Dream number two puzzles me. I am following Father, who is very small. It is not quite dark, but I don't know where the light is coming from. It is like moonlight, but without the moon, which I suspect is behind me somewhere. I am very frightened. Father starts to climb the ash tree and I retreat and watch him, growing more and more afraid but not doing anything at all, simply standing and watching as he vanishes among the leaves. I wake up in a cold sweat.

Dream number three takes place in my apartment. I am remodeling and doing the work myself. I am installing temporary wall boards, decorating them with childish pictures and pinups. I am weeping as I work. Suddenly there is a change and I am above Somerset, or in town, and I can't be certain which it is. I am calm and happy, although I see no one and hear nothing. Somerset is bathed in moonlight that is too golden to be real and the town is as I remember it from my earliest days, with striped green-and-white umbrellas in yards, and silent children playing happily in Cobb's Run.

I wake up and don't want to lose the feeling of peace and contentment. I smile as I write the dream down and when I read it over I don't know quite why it should have filled me with happiness. As I think of it more, I am saddened by it, and finally I get up wishing I had let it escape altogether. It is very early, not seven yet, but I don't want to return to bed. The morning is cool and refreshing. I decide to weed the patio out back and set up the grill before the sun heats up the valley again.

The ash tree is untouched. I work for an hour, go inside for breakfast, and return to the yard. I am thinking that if I do bring Father home, I will have to find someone who can help with the yard, and I don't know who it would be. Poor Haddie? He might, but he is so slow and unthinking. I could have a wheelchair for Father and bring him out to the patio every day and as he convalesces, we could take short trips in the car, go down to the lake maybe, or over to Hawley now and then. I am certain that he will be able to play chess by fall, and read aloud with me, as we used to do. A quiet happiness fills me as I plan and it is with surprise that I realize that I have decided about Father. I have been over the same reasoning with his doctor, and accepted his advice against this move, but here, working in the bright sunlight, the new decision seems to have been made effortlessly.

I have weeded the patio, swept up the heaps of dandelions and buckweeds and crabgrass that have pushed through the cracks in the flagstones, and set up the barbecue grill. The picnic table is in pitiful condition, but it will have to do. There are some folding canvas chairs in the garage, but I will let the boys bring them out.

It is one o'clock already. A whole morning gone so quickly. My muscles are throbbing and I am sunburned, but the feeling of peacefulness remains with me and I shower and change and then go to town to shop, have lunch with Dorothea and Annie, and then see the sleep lab equipment.

I try to explain to Dorothea the difference between living in the city and living here in my own home, but she has her mouth set in a firm line and she is very disapproving of the whole idea.

Timidly Annie says, "But, honey, there's no one left your age. What will you do all the time?"

"I'll have plenty to do," I tell her. "I want to study, rest, take care of Father, the house. There will be too much to do, probably."

"That's not what she means," Dorothea says sharply. "You should get married, not tie yourself down here where everything's dying." She eyes me appraisingly. "Don't you have anyone in mind?"

I shrug it off. A young doctor, perhaps? I try to think of myself with any of the young doctors I know, and the thought is ridiculous. There are some older doctors, thoroughly married, of course, that seem less absurd, but no one my age who is unattached. I think again of the Harvard doctor's pink hands and pink cheeks, and I shudder. I say, "There's time for that, Dorothea, but right now I feel it's my duty to Father to bring him home where he will be happier."

After lunch I wander into the parlor and have Dorothea ring Roger's room and tell him I'm waiting. She is still unhappy with me, and I know that she and Annie will discuss me the rest of the afternoon.

The sleep lab is set up in the rear of the building on the

second floor. There are three bedrooms in a row, the middle one the control room with the equipment in place, and the rooms on either side furnished with beds, telephones, wires with electrodes. I have seen pictures of these experiments and have read about them so that none of it comes as a surprise, but I am mildly impressed that they were able to get together so much equipment that I know to be very expensive. Harvard is feeling flush these days, I decide, or else Staunton swings more weight than I have given him credit for.

After I examine the EEGs from the night before and compare them with the reported dreams, I am introduced to the other three students that I missed before. I have already forgotten all of their names except Sid and Roger. We have a drink and I learn that so far they have received no cooperation from anyone in town, with the possible exception of myself. Staunton comes in looking angry and frustrated.

"That hick doctor could do it, if he would," he says before he sees me in the room. He reddens.

"He won't, though," I say. "But I could."

"They'd tell you their dreams?"

"Some of them would, probably enough for your purposes." I stand up and start for the door. "I would have to promise not to give you their dreams, but to process them myself, however."

He starts to turn away, furious again, and I say, "I am qualified, you know." I suspect that I have more degrees than he does and I reel them off rapidly. I walk to the door before he has a chance to respond. Before leaving I say, "Think about it. You can let me know tonight when you come to the house. I will have to be briefed on your methods, of course, and have a chance to examine your cards."

I don't know why I've done it. I walk home and try to find a reason, but there is none. To puncture his smug shield? To deflate him in the presence of his students? To inflate my own importance, reassure myself that I am of both worlds? I can't select a single reason, and I decide that perhaps all of them are part of it. I know that I dislike Staunton as much as anyone I have ever met, and perhaps I hope that he will fail completely in his research, except that it isn't really his.

I make potato salad, and bake pies, and prepare the steaks that Dorothea has ordered. It crosses my mind that Mr. Larson has virtually no meat except for the special order from Sagamore House, and that I'll have to order everything in advance when I move back home for good, but I don't linger over it. The evening passes quite pleasantly and even Staunton is on his good behavior. They accept my offer and Sid goes over the cards with me, explaining what they are doing, how they are analyzing the dreams and recording them. It seems simple enough.

The days flow by now, with not quite enough time for all there is to do. The doctor in charge of the nursing home answers my letter brusquely, treating me like a child. I read it over twice before I put it on my desk to be taken care of later. I have been able to get six people to cooperate in the dream studies, and they keep me busy each day. People like to talk about their dreams, I find, and talking about them, they are able to bring back more and more details, so that each interview takes half an hour or an hour. And there are my own dreams that I am also recording.

I found the reason for my own part in this when I first typed up my own dream to be analyzed. I found that I couldn't give it to Staunton, and the students are like children, not to be trusted with anything so intimate as the private dreams of a grown woman. So each day I record my own dreams along with the other six, type them all up, fill out the cards, and turn the cards over to Roger. By then the dreams are depersonalized data.

I finish typing the seven dreams and I am restless suddenly. There is something . . . The house is more unquiet than usual, and I am accustomed to the rustlings and creakings. I wonder if another storm is going to hit the town, but I don't think so.

I wander outside where the night is very clear. The sky is brilliant and bottomless. The music of the night is all about me: the splashing water of the creek, crickets and tree frogs in arrhythmic choral chants and from a distance the deeper solo bass of a bullfrog. Probably I am bored. Other people's dreams are very boring. I haven't started to categorize this latest set, and I feel reluctant to begin. I purposely don't put any names on any of the dreams I record, and I type each one on a separate card and then shuffle them about, so that by the time I have finished with them all, I have forgotten who told me which one.

I stop walking suddenly. I have come halfway down the path toward the creek without thinking where I am going or why. Now I stop and the night noises press in on me. "They are alike," I say, and I am startled by my voice. All other sounds stop with the words.

I think of the stack of file cards, and those I added tonight, and I am amazed that I didn't see it in the beginning. Roger is right: the townspeople are dreaming the same dreams. That isn't really what he said. What he said was that the dreams of the people here would remain stable, unchanged by the experiment, while those of the students would change as they adapted to this life. I haven't asked about that part of the research, but suddenly I am too curious about it to put it out of my mind.

Are they changing, and how? I start back, but pause at the door to the house, and turn instead to the street and town. I slow down when I come in sight of Sagamore House. It is very late, almost two in the morning. The second-floor light is the only light I have seen since leaving my own house. I take another step toward Sagamore House, and another. What is the matter tonight? I look about. But there is nothing. No wind, no moon, nothing. But I hear . . . life, stirrings, something. This is Somerset, I say to myself sharply, not quite aloud, but I hear the words anyway. I look quickly over my shoulder, but there is nothing. I see the apple trees, familiar yet strange, eerie shadows against the pale siding of the hotel. Across from Sagamore House on

Wisteria there is the old boarded-up theater, and for a moment I think someone has opened it again. I press my hands over my ears and when I take them down the sound has stopped. I am shaking. I can't help the sudden look that I give the corner where the drugstore burned down seven or eight years ago.

We wait in the shadows of Sagamore House, under the apple trees for the movie to be over, and then Father and Mother, Susan's parents, Peter's, come out and take us along with them for an ice-cream soda in the drugstore. We know when the movie is ending because of the sounds that filter out when they open the inner doors. Faint music, laughter, a crash of cymbals, always different, but always a signal, and we come down from the trees, or from the porch and cross the street to wait for them to come out.

I stare at the theater, back to the empty corner, and slowly turn and go home again. One of the boys was playing a radio, I tell myself, and even believe it for a moment. Or I imagined it, the past intruded for a moment, somehow. An audio hallucination. I stop at the gate to my yard and stare at the house, and I am desperately afraid. It is such an unfamiliar feeling, so unexpected and shattering, that I can't move until it passes. It is as if I have become someone else for a moment, someone who fears rustling in the dark, who fears the night, being alone. Not my feelings at all. I have never been afraid, never, not of anything like this.

I light a cigarette and walk around the house to enter the kitchen, where I make coffee and a sandwich. It is two-thirty, but sleep seems a long way off now, unwanted, unneeded. Toward dawn I take a sleeping pill and fall into bed.

Roger, Sid and Doug invite me to have dinner with them in Hawley on Saturday, and I accept. The mountain road is very bad and we creep along in the station wagon that they have brought with them. No one is talking, and we all glance back at Somerset at the turn that used to have a tended scenic overlook. The trees have since grown up, and bushes and vines, so that there is only a hint of the town below us. Then it is gone, and suddenly Sid starts to talk of the experiment.

"I think we should call off the rest of it," he says.

"Can't," Roger says. "Eight days isn't enough."

"We have a trend," Sid says.

Doug, sitting in the back seat, speaks up then. "You'll never keep them all here for two more weeks."

"I know that, but those who do hang on will be enough."

"What's the matter?" I ask.

"Boredom," Sid says. "Good God, what's there to do in such a place?"

"I thought that was part of the experiment. I thought you wanted a place with no external stimuli."

"Quote and unquote," Sid says. "Staunton's idea. And we did, but I don't know. The dreams are strange, and getting stranger. And we're not getting along too well in the daytime. I don't know how your people stand it."

I shrug and don't even try to answer. I know he won't understand. Traffic thickens when we leave the secondary road for the highway on the other side of the mountain. It feels cooler here and I find that I am looking forward to a night out with more excitement than seems called for.

We have drinks before dinner, and wine with dinner, and more drinks afterward, and there is much laughter. Doug teaches me three new dance steps, and Roger and I dance, and I find myself thinking with incredulity of the plan I have been considering to take Father out of the nursing home where he belongs and try to care for him myself. I know that he will never recover, that he will become more and more helpless, not less. How could I have planned to do such a thing? He needs attendants to lift him, turn him in bed, and at times to restrain him. I have tried to think of other alternatives for him, but there are none, and I know that. I know that I have to write to the director of the home and apologize to him.

At eleven Roger says we have to go back. Doug passes out in

Somerset Dreams 29

the car as soon as he gets inside, and Sid groans. "There he goes," he says. "So you do me tonight."

"Where are the others?" I ask.

"On strike," Roger says. "They refused to work on Saturday and Sunday, said they needed time off. They want to forget their dreams for a couple of nights."

"I'll do it," I say.

"You're kidding."

"No. I'll do it. You can wire me up and everything tonight."

It is agreed, and we drive back over the mountain, becoming more and more quiet as we get to the old road and start to pick our way down again. By the time we get back to Somerset, and I am feeling soberer, I regret my impulsive promise, but can think of no way to back out now. I watch Sid and Roger half carry, half drag Doug from the station wagon, and I see the flutter of his eyelids and know that he is not as drunk as he would have us believe. I start to walk to my house, but Roger says for me to wait, that they will drive me and bring me back with my pajamas and things, so I stand on the porch and wait for them, and I stare across the street at the vacant theater. I know that three nights ago I imagined the past, but since then I have been taking sleeping pills, and my nights have been quiet, with no more hallucinations or dreams.

My house is noisier than usual. I glance at the two boys, but neither of them seems to notice. They sit in the living room and wait, and ahead of me on the dark stairs the rustlings hurry along; they pause outside my parents' room, scurry down the hallway and precede me into my room, where, when I turn on the light, there is nothing to see. I know it is the settling of floorboards untrodden for eleven months; and rushing air; and imagination. Memories that have become tangible? I don't believe that, but it has a strangely comforting sound, and I like the idea of memories lingering in the house, assuming a life of their own, reliving the past.

I fold pajamas and my housecoat, and grope under the bed

for my slippers, and the thought comes that people are going
to know that I spent the night at Sagamore House. I sit on the
bed with my slippers in my hand and stare straight ahead at
nothing in particular. How can I get out of this? I realize that
Somerset and New York are arguing through me, and I can
almost smile at the dialogue that I am carrying out silently. It
seems that my strongest Somerset argument is that if I am going
to live here with my invalid father, I can't return with a reputa-
tion completely ruined. I know what Somerset can do to a
woman like that. But I'm not going to come back with him, I
answer. Or am I?

It is getting very late and I have to go through with it; I have
promised. Reluctantly I take my things downstairs, hoping that
they have left, but of course they are still sitting there, talking
quietly. About me? I suspect so. Probably I puzzle them. I
regard them as little more than children, boys with school problems to solve. Yet we are all in our twenties. I suppose that
because I have my degrees and a position of responsibility, my
experience seems to add years to my age, and even as I think
this, I reject it. Sid has told me that he spent three years in the
army, served in Vietnam, so what is my experience to his? Sid
has tried to draw me out, has visited twice, and has even gone
canoeing with me, but standing in the doorway looking at them
I think of them as so very young, prying into things they can't
understand, trying to find answers that, if found, will make
them question all of reality. I shake my head hard. I don't know
what I've been thinking about, but I feel afraid suddenly, and
I suspect that I have drunk too much earlier, and I am so very
. . . weary. Sleeping pills leave me more tired than the insomnia
they alleviate.

They make small talk that I recognize, the same sort of small
talk that a good doctor uses for a nervous patient before measur-
ing his blood pressure. I am churlish with them in return and
we go to the sleep lab silently. I understand all of their equipment and I have even had electroencephalograms made when

I was studying, so nothing is new to me and the demonstration is short. Then I am alone in the darkened room, conscious of the wires, of the tiny patches of skin with adhesive gel tape that holds the electrodes in place. I don't think I'll be able to go to sleep here wired up like this, at least not into the deep sleep that should come in an hour or so. I deliberately close my eyes and try to picture a flame above my eyes, over the bridge of my nose. I know that I can interrupt my alpha waves at will with this exercise. I imagine Roger's surprise. But suddenly I am thinking of S.L. and I blink rapidly, wondering what kinds of waves I am producing now for them to study. S.L. won't go away. I ask, what does the S. stand for, and he smiles broadly and says Silas. Does anyone name children Silas any more? So I ask about the L. and he says Lerner, which is perfectly all right, his mother's maiden name, but he doesn't like the idea of going around as S. Lerner Wright. It is a farcical name. He is S.L. Lying in the dark room of the almost empty hotel, I can think of S.L. without pain, without recriminations and regrets and bitterness. I remember it as it was then. I loved him so very much, but he said not enough, or I would go with him to Cal Tech and become Mrs. S.L. Wright, and forever and ever remain Mrs. S.L. Wright. I realize that I no longer love him, and that probably I didn't even then, but it felt like love and I ached as if it were love, and afterward I cut my hair very short and stopped using makeup and took several courses in night school and finished the next three years in under two and received degrees and a job . . .

I am awakened by the telephone and I lift it and mumble into it. "My car isn't working right, trying to back up on the road into Somerset and can't make it go. I keep slipping downward and there is a cliff in front of me, but I can't back up."

I dream of the telephone ringing, and it rings, and I speak, less coherently, and forget immediately what I have said and sleep again. In the morning I have memories of having spoken into the telephone several times, but no memories of what I said. Sid enters and helps me out of the bird's nest of wires. I wave him away and stumble into the bathroom where I wash my face and come really awake.

Sid? I thought Roger was the meter man of the night before. I dress and brush my hair and put on lipstick, and then find them both waiting for me to have breakfast with them. Sid has deep blue circles under his eyes. At a sunlit table with a bowl of yellow roses and a few deep green ferns. I wait for them to break the silence that has enveloped the three of us. There is a sound of activity in town that morning, people getting ready to go to church in Hawley, cars being brought out of garages where they stay six days of the week, several people in the hotel dining room having an early breakfast before leaving for the day. Many of them stay away all day on Sunday, visiting friends or relatives, and I know that later the town will be deserted.

"So they talked you into letting them wire you up like a condemned man?" Dorothea stands over the table accusingly. "Are you all right?"

"Of course. It's nothing, Dorothea, really nothing."

She snorts. "Up all night, people coming and going all night, talking in the halls, meetings here and there. I never should have let them in." She is addressing me still, but the hostility in her voice is aimed at the boys, at Staunton, who has just entered the dining room. He joins us, and there are dark hollows under his eyes. He doesn't meet my gaze.

We have coffee in silence and wait for our orders. I finger a sensitive spot on my left eyelid and Sid says quickly, "One of the wires came off during the night. I had to replace it. Is it sore?"

"No. It's all right." I am upset suddenly by the idea of his being there in the night, replacing a wire on my eye without my knowing. I think of the similar role that I play in my daily life and I know how I regard the bodies that I treat. Irritated at the arm that has managed to pull loose a needle that now must be replaced in the vein. Never a person, just an arm, and a needle. And the quiet satisfaction when the dials are registering correctly once more. I feel the frown on my face and try to smooth it out again.

Staunton has ordered only toast, juice and coffee, and he is yawning. He finishes his last crumb of toast and says, "I'm going to bed. Miss Matthews, will you join us here for dinner tonight?"

The sudden question catches me off guard, and I look at him. He is regarding me steadily and very soberly, and I realize that something has happened, that I am part of it, and that he is very much concerned. I am uneasy and only nod yes.

When he is gone I ask, "What happened? What's wrong?"

"We don't know yet," Roger says.

Sid pours more coffee and drinks it black. He is looking more awake, as if he has taken a bennie or something. "We have to talk with you, Janet. I'd like you to hear some of our tapes, including your own, if you will."

"You should get some sleep," I say irrelevantly.

"This afternoon? Can you come here, or should we bring the stuff to your place?"

"You got him up last night?"

Roger nods. "I felt I should."

I watch Myra and Al Newton leave their table, stop at Dorothea's counter to pay the bill and leave, and I am struck by their frailty. They both seem wraithlike. Is anyone in Somerset under sixty? I suppose the Newtons must be closer to seventy-five. I ask, "Where are the other boys this morning?" The dining room is empty except for the three of us.

"A couple of them are out fishing already, and the rest are probably still sleeping. I'm taking Victor and Mickey to Hawley to catch the bus back to Boston later today," Roger says, and then adds, "Probably Doug will be the next to go."

"Doug? I thought he was one of the more interested ones in this whole thing?"

"Too interested, maybe," Roger says.

Sid is watching both of us and now he leans forward, resting his chin on his hands, looking beyond me out the window at the quiet street. "Janet, do you remember any of your dreams from last night?"

I think of what I said over the telephone. Scraps here and there. Something about putting flowers on graves in one of them. I shake my head: nothing that I can really remember.

"Okay. You'll hear them later. Meanwhile, take my word for it that some of the guys have to leave, whether they want to or not." He looks at me for another moment and then asks, in a different voice altogether, "Are you all right, Janet? Will you be okay until this afternoon? We do have to process the tapes and record the data, and I want to sort through all of them and pull out those that seem pertinent."

It is the voice of a man concerned for a woman, not of a graduate student concerned for his project, and this annoys me.

"Of course I'm all right," I say, and stand up. "For heaven's sake, those are dreams, the dreams of someone who had too much to drink, at that." I know I am flushed and I turn to leave. Have I embarrassed them with erotic dreams, concerning one of them perhaps? I am very angry when I leave Sagamore House, and I wish I could go up to the sleep room and destroy the tapes, all of them. I wish Dorothea had shown just an ounce of sense when they approached her for the rooms. She had no business allowing them to come into our town, upset our people with their damned research. I am furious with Sid for showing concern for me. He has no right. In the middle of these thoughts, I see my father and me, walking hand in hand in the afternoon, heading for the drugstore and an ice-cream cone. He is very tall and blond, with broad shoulders and a massive chest. He keeps his hair so short that he seems bald from a distance. He is an ophthalmologist with his office in Jefferson, and after they dam the river he has to drive sixty-three miles each way. Mother worries about his being out so much, but they don't move, don't even consider moving. On Sunday afternoon he always takes me to the drugstore for an ice-cream cone. I blink hard and the image fades, leaving the street bare and empty.

I am too restless to remain in my house. It is a hot still day and the heat is curling the petals of the roses, and drying out the grass, and wilting the phlox leaves. It is a relentless sun, burning, broiling, sucking the water up from the creek, leaving it smaller each day. Without the dam the creek probably would dry up completely within another week or two. I decide to cut a basket of flowers and take them to the cemetery, and I know the idea comes from the fragmentary dream that I recalled earlier. I haven't been to the cemetery since my mother's funeral. It has always seemed such a meaningless gesture, to return to a grave and mourn there. It is no less meaningless now, but it is something to do.

The cemetery is behind the small white church that has not been used for six years, since Brother MacCombs died. No one tried to replace him; they seemed tacitly to agree that the church should be closed and the membership transferred to Hawley.

It is a walk of nearly two miles, past the Greening farm where the weeds have become master again, past the dirt road to the old mill, a tumbling ruin even in my childhood where snakes curled in the shadows and slept, past the turnoff to Eldridge's fishing camp. I see no one and the sounds of the hot summer day are loud about me: whirring grasshoppers, birds, the scuttling of a squirrel who chatters at me once he is safely hidden.

The cemetery is tended in spots only, the graves of those whose relatives are still in Somerset have cut grass and a sprinkling of flowers. My mother's grave is completely grown over and shame fills me. What would Father say? I don't try to weed it then, but sit down under a wide oak tree.

I look at the narrow road that leads back to Somerset. Father and I will come here often, after I have made the grave neat and pretty again. It will be slow, but we'll take our time, walking hand in hand up the dirt road, carrying flowers, and maybe a sandwich and a thermos of lemonade, or apples. Probably if I start the proceedings during the coming week, I can have everything arranged by next weekend, hire an ambulance and a driver . . .

I am awakened by rough hands shaking my shoulders. I blink rapidly, trying to focus my eyes, trying to find myself. I am being led away, and I squirm to turn around because I feel so certain that I am still back there somehow. I almost catch a glimpse of a girl in a yellow dress, sitting with her back to the oak tree, but it shimmers and I am yanked hard, and stumble, and hands catch me and steady me.

"What are you kids doing?" I ask, and the sound of the voice, deep, unfamiliar, shocks me and only then do I really wake up. I am being taken to the station wagon that is parked at the entrance to the lane.

"I'm all right," I say, not struggling now. "You woke me up."

Sid is on my right and Roger on my left. I see that Dr. Staunton is in the wagon. He looks pale and worried.

I remember the basket of flowers that I never did put on the grave and I look back once more to see it standing by the tree. Sid's hand tightens on my arm, but I don't try to pull away. Inside the wagon I say, "Will one of you tell me what that was all about?"

"Janet, do you know how long you've been there at the cemetery?"

"Half an hour, an hour."

"It's almost six now. I . . . we got to your house at three and waited awhile for you, and then went back to the hotel. An old man with a white goatee said he saw you before noon heading this way with flowers. So we came after you." Sid is sitting beside me in the back seat of the wagon, and I stare at him in disbelief. I look at my watch, and it is five minutes to six. I shake it and listen to it.

"I must have been sound asleep."

"Sitting straight up, with your legs stretched out in front of you?"

We drive to my house and I go upstairs to wash my face and

comb my hair. I study my face carefully, looking for something, anything, but it is the same. I hear voices from below; the sound diminishes and I know they are playing the tapes, so I hurry down.

I see that Sid has found my dream cards, the typed reports, and I am angry with him for prying. He says, "I had to know. I found them earlier while we were waiting for you."

Roger has the tape ready, so I sit down and we listen for the next two hours. Staunton is making notes, scowling hard at the pad on his knee. I feel myself growing tenser, and when the first tape comes to an end, I go to make coffee. We all sip it through the playing of the second tape.

The dreaming students' voices sound disjointed, hesitant, unguarded, and the dreams they relate are all alike. I feel cold in the hot room, and I dread hearing my own voice, my own dreams played by the machine.

All the early dreams are of attempts to leave Somerset. They speak of trying to fly out, to climb out, to swim out, to drive out, and only one is successful. As the night progresses, the dreams change, some faster than others. Slowly a pattern of acceptance enters the dreams, and quite often the acceptance is followed swiftly by a nightmarelike desire to run.

One of the dreamers, Victor, I think it is, has a brief anxiety dream, an incomplete dream, and then nothing but the wish-fulfillment acceptance dreams, not even changing again when morning has him in a lighter stage of sleep.

Sid motions for Roger to stop the tape and says, "That was three days ago. Since then Victor has been visiting people here, talking with them, fishing, hiking. He has been looking over some of the abandoned houses in town, with the idea of coming here to do a book."

"Has he . . ." I am amazed at how dry my mouth has become and I have to sip cold coffee before I can ask the question. "Has he recorded dreams since then?"

"No. Before this, he was having dreams of his parents, caring

for them, watching over them." Sid looks at me and says deliberately, "Just like your dreams."

I shake my head and turn from him to look at Roger. He starts
the machine again. There are hours and hours of the tapes to
hear, and after another fifteen minutes of them I am ravenous.
It is almost nine. I signal Roger to stop, and suggest that we all
have scrambled eggs here, but Staunton vetoes this.

"I promised Miss Dorothea that we would return to the hotel.
I warned her that it might be late. She said that was all right."

So we go back to Sagamore House and wait for the special of
the day. On Sunday night there is no menu. I find myself shying
away from the implications of the dream analysis again and
again, and try to concentrate instead on my schedule for the
next several months. I know that I have agreed to work with Dr.
Waldbaum on at least six operations, and probably there are
others that I agreed to and have forgotten. He is a thoracic
surgeon and his operations take from four to eight or even ten
hours, and for that long I control death, keep life in abeyance.
I pay no attention to the talk that is going on between Roger
and Sid, and I wonder about getting an ambulance driver to
bring Father in during the winter. If only our weather were
more predictable; there might be snowdrifts six feet high on the
road, or it might be balmy.

"I said, why do you think you should bring your father home,
here to Somerset?" I find that my eyes are on Staunton, and
obviously he thinks I have been listening to him, but the question takes me by surprise.

"He's my father. He needs me."

Sid asks, "Has anyone in town encouraged you in this idea?"

Somehow, although I have tried to withdraw from them, I am
again the center of their attention, and I feel uncomfortable
and annoyed. "Of course not. This is my decision alone. Dr.
Warren tried to discourage it, in fact, as Dorothea did, and Mr.
Larson."

"Same thing," Sid says to Roger, who nods. Staunton looks at
them and turns to me.

"Miss Matthews, do you mean to say that everyone you've talked to about this has really tried to discourage it? These people are your father's friends. Why would they do that?"

My face feels stiff and I am thinking that this is too much, but I say, "They all seem to think he's better off in the nursing home."

"And isn't he?"

"In certain respects, yes. But I am qualified to handle him, you know. No one here seems to realize just how well qualified I really am. They think of me as the girl they used to know playing jump rope in the back yard."

Dorothea brings icy cucumber soup and we are silent until she leaves again. The grandfather clock chimes ten, and I am amazed at how swiftly the day has gone. By now most of the townspeople are either in bed, or getting ready. Sunday is a hard day, with the trip to church, visits, activities that they don't have often enough to become accustomed to. They will sleep well tonight, I think. I look at Sid and think that he should sleep well too tonight. His eyes are sunken-looking, and I suppose he has lost weight; he looks older, more mature than he did the first time I met him.

"Are you going to set up your equipment tonight?" I ask. "Any of the other boys volunteer?"

"No," Roger says shortly. He looks at Sid and says, "As a matter of fact, we decided today not to put any of them in it again here."

"You're leaving then?"

"Sending all the kids back, but Sid and I'll be staying for a while. And Dr. Staunton,"

I put down my spoon and lean back, waiting for something that is implicit in the way Roger stops and Sid looks murderously at him. I watch Sid now.

"We think you should leave, too," he says.

I look to Roger, who nods, and then at Staunton. He is so petulant-looking, even pursing his lips. He fidgets and says, "Miss Matthews, may I suggest something? You won't take it

amiss?" I simply wait. He goes on, "I think you should return
to the city and make an appointment with the psychiatrist at
Columbia."

"And the others you are sending out? Should they also see
doctors?"

"As a matter of fact, I do think so."

Sid is examining his bowl of soup with great care, and Roger
is having trouble with his cigarette lighter. "But not them?" I
ask Staunton, pointing at Roger and Sid.

"Them too," he says reluctantly. Sid looks amused now and
Roger manages to light his cigarette.

"Is this your opinion too?" I ask Sid. "That I should see Dr.
Calridge?"

"No. Just go away from here, and stay away."

Dorothea is bringing in a cart now and I wonder how much
she has heard. I see her lined face and the pain in her eyes and
I know that she has heard a lot of it, if not all. She catches my
gaze and nods firmly. Then she serves us: sizzling ham steaks,
french fried fruits, pineapple, apple rings, bananas, sweet potato soufflé.

It is after eleven when we are finished with dinner, and by
now Sid is almost asleep. He says, "I've got to go. Will you set
things up, Rog?"

"Sure. Damn shame that Doug pooped out on us. We need
all the data we can get now."

"I can do the recording," I say.

At almost the same instant Staunton says, "I thought I was
going to record both of you tonight."

Roger and Sid look embarrassed, and Sid says after a pause,
"Dr. Staunton, if it's all the same with you, we'll let Janet do
it."

"You really think I'm that biased? That I can't get objective
data?"

Sid stands up and steadies himself with one hand on the table.
"I'm too tired to be polite," he says, "and too tired to argue. So,

yes, I think you're too biased to record the dreams. Roger, will you show Janet what we're doing?"

Roger stays with me until the eye-movement trace shows that Sid is having his first dream, and he watches as I call Sid on the phone and turn on the recorder, and then switch it off again. Then Roger goes to bed in the second room and I see that his electrodes are all working, and I am alone watching the two sets of moving lines. The mountains and valleys of life, I think, watching them peak and level out, and peak again.

There is no mistaking the start of REM sleep; the rapid eye movements cause a sharp change in the pattern of the peaks and valleys that is more nearly like a waking EEG than that of a sleeping person. I call Sid again, and listen to him describe climbing a mountain, only to slip back down again and again. Roger is on a raft that keeps getting caught up on a tide and brought back to a shore that he is desperately trying to escape.

The same dream, different only in details. Like the dreams I heard earlier on the tape recorder. Like my own.

At three in the morning Staunton joins me. I can tell that he hasn't been asleep, but I wish he had kept his insomnia to himself. He says, "You might need help. I won't bother you. I'll just sit over here and read." He looks haggard, and like Sid, he seems to have aged since coming to Somerset. I turn my attention to the EEGs again. Roger is dreaming.

"Peaceful now, watching a ball game from a great distance, very silent everywhere." I bite my lips as I listen to this strange voice that seems to have a different accent, a different intonation; flatter and slower, of course, but apart from that, it is a changed voice. It is the dream of contentment, wanting nothing, needing nothing. This is the dream that my six people keep reporting to me, modified from person to person, but the same. Suddenly Roger's voice sharpens as he recalls the rest of the dream, and now there is a sense of urgency in his reporting. "And I had to get out of it, but couldn't move. I was frozen there, watching the game, afraid of something I couldn't see, but knew was right behind me. Couldn't move."

I glance at Staunton and he is staring at the moving pens. Roger has become silent once more, so I turn off the tape recorder and look also at the continuing record. Typical nightmare pattern.

Staunton yawns and I turn to him and say, "Why don't you try to get some sleep? Really, I'm fine. I slept almost all day, remember?"

He yawns again, then says, "If . . . if I seem to be dreaming, will you waken me?" I nod and he stretches out on the couch and is asleep almost instantly.

There is a coffee maker with strong coffee hot in it, and I pour myself a cup, and try to read the book that Roger provided, a spy thriller. I can't keep my mind on it. The hotel is no more noisy at night than my own house, but the noises are not the same, and I find myself listening to them, rustlings in the halls, distant doors opening and closing, the occasional squeak of the porch swing. I sit up straighter. A woman's laugh? Not at three-fifteen in the morning, surely. I have more coffee and wander to the window. A light on in the Sayer house? I blink and when I look again, I know that it was my imagination. I remember how their baby used to keep night hours, and smile. The baby would be fifteen or sixteen now, at least. I used to baby-sit for them now and then, and the child never slept.

I return to my chair by the electroencephalograph and see that Sid has started a new dream. I reach for the phone, waiting for the peak to level off again, and slowly withdraw my hand. He is dreaming a long one this time. After five minutes I begin to feel uneasy, but still I wait. Roger has said to rouse the sleeper after ten minutes of dreaming, if he hasn't shown any sign of being through by then. I wait, and suddenly jerk awake and stab my finger at the phone button. He doesn't answer.

I forget to turn on the recorder, but rush into the next room to bring him out of this dream turned into nightmare, and when I touch his shoulder, I am in it too.

Somerset is gay and alive with playing children, and sun umbrellas everywhere. There are tables on the lawn of Sagamore House, and ladies in long white skirts moving among them, laughing happily. The Governor is due and Dorothea and Annie are bustling about, ordering the girls in black aprons this way and that, and everywhere there is laughter. A small boy approaches the punch bowl with a wriggling frog held tightly in one hand, and he is caught and his knickers are pulled down summarily and the sounds of hand on bottom are plainly heard, followed by wails. I am so busy, and someone keeps trying to pull me away and talk to me. I shake him off and run to the table where Father and Mother are sitting, and see to it that they have punch, and then swirl back to the kitchen where Dorothea is waiting for me to help her with the ice sculpture that is the centerpiece. It is a tall boy with curly hair rising up from a block of ice, the most beautiful thing I've ever seen, and I want to weep for him because in a few hours he will be gone. I slip on a piece of ice and fall, fall . . . fall . . .

I catch the wires attached to Sid and pull them loose, half pull him from the bed, and we end up in a heap. He holds me tightly for a long time, until we are both breathing normally again, and my shaking has stopped, and his too.

There is pale dawnlight in the room. Enough to see that his dark hair is damp with sweat, and curly on his forehead. He pushes it back and very gently moves me aside and disentangles himself from the wires.

"We have to get out of here," he says.

Staunton is sound asleep on the couch, breathing deeply but normally, and Roger is also sleeping. His graph shows that he has had nightmares several times.

We take our coffee into the room where Sid slept, and sit at the window drinking it, watching morning come to Somerset. I say, "They don't know, do they?"

"Of course not."

Poor Haddie appears at the far end of the street, walking

toward Mr. Larson's store. He shuffles his feet as he moves, never lifting them more than an inch. I shudder and turn away.

"Isn't there something that we should do? Report this, or something?"

"Who would believe it? Staunton doesn't, and he has seen it over and over this week."

A door closes below us and I know Dorothea is up now, in the kitchen starting coffee. "I was in her dream, I think," I say.

I look down into my cup and think of the retirement villages all over the south, and again I shiver. "They seem so accepting, so at peace with themselves, just waiting for the end." I shake the last half inch of coffee back and forth. I ask, "Is that what happened with me? Did I not want to wake up?"

Sid nods. "I was taking the electrodes off your eyes when you snapped out of it, but yours wasn't a nightmare. It just wouldn't end. That's what frightened me, that it wasn't a nightmare. You didn't seem to be struggling against it at all. I wonder what brought you out of it this time."

I remember the gleaming ice sculpture, the boy with curly hair who will be gone so soon, and I know why I fought to get away. Someday I think probably I'll tell him, but not now, not so soon. The sun is high and the streets are bright now. I stand up. "I'm sorry that I forgot to turn on the tape recorder and ask you right away what the dream was. Do you remember it now?"

He hesitates only a moment and then shakes his head. Maybe someday he'll tell me, but not now, not so soon.

I leave him and find Dorothea waiting for me in the parlor. She draws me inside and shuts the door and takes a deep breath. "Janet, I am telling you that you must not bring your father back here to stay. It would be the worst possible thing for you to do."

I can't speak for a moment, but I hug her, and try not to see her etched face and the white hair, but to see her as she was when she was still in long skirts, with pretty pink cheeks and sparkling eyes. I can't manage it. "I know," I say finally. "I know."

Walking home again, hot in the sunlight, listening to the rustlings of Somerset, imagining the unseen life that flits here and there out of my line of vision, I wonder if memories can become tangible, live a life of their own. I will pack, I think, and later in the day drive back up the mountain, back to the city, but not back to my job. Not back to administering death, even temporary death. Perhaps I shall go into psychiatry, or research psychology. As I begin to pack, my house stirs with movement.

The Encounter

THE BUS SLID to an uneasy stop, two hours late. Snow was eight inches deep, and the white sky met the white ground in a strange world where the grubby black bus station floated free. It was a world where up and down had become meaningless, where the snow fell horizontally. Crane, supported by the wind and the snow, could have entered the station by walking up the wall, or across the ceiling. His mind seemed adrift, out of touch with the reality of his body. He stamped, scattering snow, bringing some feeling back to his legs, making himself feel the floor beneath his feet. He tried to feel his cheek, to see if he was feverish, but his hands were too numb, his cheek too numb. The heating system of the bus had failed over an hour ago.

The trouble was that he had not dressed for such weather. An overcoat, but no boots, no fur-lined gloves, no woolen scarf to wind and wind about his throat. He stamped and clapped his hands. Others were doing the same.

There had been only nine or ten people on the bus, and some of them were being greeted by others or were slipping out into the storm, home finally or near enough now. The bus driver was talking to an old man who had been in the bus station when they arrived, the ticket agent, probably. He was wearing two sweaters, one heavy, hip-length green that looked home-knit; under it, a turtleneck gray wool with too-long sleeves that hung from beneath the green sleeves. He had on furry boots that came to his knees, with his sagging pants tucked tightly into them. Beyond him, tossed over one of the wooden benches, was a greatcoat, fleece-lined, long enough to hang to his boot tops. Fleecy gloves bulged from one of the pockets.

"Folks," he said, turning away from the bus driver, "there won't be another bus until sometime in the morning, when they get the roads plowed out some. There's an all-night diner down the road, three-four blocks. Not much else in town's open this time of night."

"Is there a hotel?" A woman, fur coat, shiny patent boots, kid gloves. She had got on at the same station that Crane had; he remembered the whiff of expensive perfume as she had passed him.

"There's the Laughton Inn, ma'am, but it's two miles outside town and there's no way to get there."

"Oh, for God's sake! You mean this crummy burg doesn't even have a hotel of its own?"

"Four of them, in fact, but they're closed, open again in April. Don't get many people to stay overnight in the wintertimes."

"Okay, okay. Which way's the diner?" She swept a disapproving glance over the bleak station and went to the door, carrying an overnight bag with her.

"Come on, honey. I'm going there, too," the driver said. He pulled on gloves and turned up his collar. He took her arm firmly, transferred the bag to his other hand, then turned to look at the other three or four people in the station. "Anyone else?"

Diner. Glaring lights, jukebox noise without end, the smell of hamburgers and onions, rank coffee and doughnuts saturated with grease. Everyone smoking. Someone would have cards probably, someone a bottle. The woman would sing or cry, or get a fight going. She was a nasty one, he could tell. She'd be bored within an hour. She'd have the guys groping her under the table, in the end booth. The man half-turned, his back shielding her from view, his hand slipping between her buttons, under the blouse, under the slip, the slippery smooth nylon, the tightness of the bra, unfastening it with his other hand. Her low laugh, busy hands. The hard nipple between his fingers now, his own responsive hardness. She had turned to look at the stranded passengers when the driver spoke, and she caught Crane's glance.

"It's a long wait for a Scranton bus, honey," she said.

"I'd just get soaked going to the diner," Crane said, and turned his back on her. His hand hurt, and he opened his clenched fingers and rubbed his hands together hard.

"I sure as hell don't want to wait all night in this rathole," someone else said. "Do you have lockers? I can't carry all this gear."

"Lock them up in the office for you," the ticket agent said. He pulled out a bunch of keys and opened a door at the end of the room. A heavyset man followed him, carrying three suitcases. They returned; the door squeaked. The agent locked it again.

"Now, you boys will hold me up, won't you? I don't want to fall down in all that snow."

"Doll, if you fall on your pretty little ass, I'll dry you off personally," the driver said.

"Oh, you will, will you?"

Crane tightened his jaw, trying not to hear them. The outside door opened and a blast of frigid air shook the room. A curtain of snow swept across the floor before the door banged again, and the laughing voices were gone.

"You sure you want to wait here?" the ticket agent asked. "Not very warm in here. And I'm going home in a minute, you know."

"I'm not dressed to walk across the street in this weather, much less four blocks," Crane said.

The agent still hesitated, one hand on his coat. He looked

around, as if checking on loose valuables. There was a woman
on one of the benches. She was sitting with her head lowered,
hands in her lap, legs crossed at the ankles. She wore a dark
cloth coat, and her shoes were skimpier than Crane's, three
crossing strips of leather attached to paper-thin soles. Black
cloth gloves hid her hands. She didn't look up, in the silence that
followed, while the two men scrutinized her. It was impossible
to guess her age in that pose, with only the dark clothes to go
by.

"Ma'am, are you all right?" the agent asked finally.

"Yes, of course. Like the gentleman, I didn't care to wade
through the snow. I can wait here."

She raised her head and with a touch of disappointment
Crane saw that she was as nondescript as her clothing. When he
stopped looking at her, he couldn't remember what she looked
like. A woman. Thirty. Thirty-five. Forty. He didn't know. And
yet. There was something vaguely familiar about her, as if he
should remember her, as if he might have seen her or met her
at one time or another. He had a very good memory for faces
and names, an invaluable asset for a salesman, and he searched
his memory for this woman and came up with nothing.

"Don't you have nothing with you that you could change
into?" the agent asked peevishly. "You'd be more comfortable
down at the diner."

"I don't have anything but some work with me," she said. Her
voice was very patient. "I thought I'd be in the city before the
storm came. Late bus, early storm. I'll be fine here."

Again his eyes swept through the dingy room, searching for
something to say, not finding anything. He began to pull on his
coat, and he seemed to gain forty pounds. "Telephone under
the counter, back there," he said finally. "Pay phone's outside
under a drift, I reckon."

"Thank you," she said.

The agent continued to dawdle. He pulled on his gloves,
checked the rest rooms to make sure the doors were not locked,

that the lights worked. He peered at a thermostat, muttering that you couldn't believe what it said anyways. At the door he stopped once more. He looked like a walking heap of outdoor garments, a clothes pile that had swallowed a man. "Mr.—uh—"

"Crane. Randolph Crane. Manhattan."

"—Uh, yes. Mr. Crane, I'll tell the troopers that you two are up here. And the road boys. Plow'll be out soon's it lets up some. They'll keep an eye open for you, if you need anything. Maybe drop in with some coffee later on."

"Great," Crane said. "That'd be great."

"Okay, then. I wouldn't wander out if I was you. See you in the morning, then. Night."

The icy blast and the inrushing snow made Crane start to shake again. He looked over at the woman who was huddling down, trying to wrap herself up in the skimpy coat.

His shivering eased, and he sat down and opened his briefcase and pulled out one of the policies he had taken along to study. This was the first time he had touched it. He hoped the woman would fall asleep and stay asleep until the bus came in the morning. He knew that he wouldn't be able to stretch out on the short benches, not that it would matter anyway. He wasn't the type to relax enough to fall asleep anywhere but in bed.

He stared at the policy, a twenty-year endowment, two years to go to maturity, on the life of William Sanders, age twenty-two. He held it higher, trying to catch the light, but the print was a blur; all he could make out were the headings of the clauses, and these he already knew by heart. He turned the policy over; it was the same on the back, the old familiar print, and the rest a blur. He started to refold the paper to return it to the briefcase. She would think he was crazy, taking it out, looking at it a moment, turning it this way and that, and then putting it back. He pursed his lips and pretended to read.

Sanders, Sanders. What did he want? Four policies, the endowment, a health and accident, a straight life, and a mortgage policy. Covered, protected. Insurance-poor, Sanders had said, throwing the bulky envelope onto Crane's desk. "Consolidate these things somehow. I want cash if I can get it, and out from under the rest."

"But what about your wife, the kids?"

"Ex-wife. If I go, she'll manage. Let her carry insurance on me."

Crane had been as persuasive as he knew how to be, and in the end he had had to promise to assess the policies, to have figures to show cash values, and so on. Disapprovingly, of course.

"You know, dear, you really are getting more stuffy every day," Mary Louise said.

"And if he dies, and his children are left destitute, then will I be so stuffy?"

"I'd rather have the seven hundred dollars myself than see it go to your company year after year."

"That's pretty shortsighted."

"Are you really going to wear that suit to Maggie's party?"

"Changing the subject?"

"Why not? You know what you think, and I know what I think, and they aren't even within hailing distance of each other."

Mary Louise wore a red velvet gown that was slit to her navel, molded just beneath her breasts by a silver chain, and almost completely bare in the back, down to the curve of her buttocks. The silver chain cut into her tanned back slightly. Crane stared at it.

"New?"

"Yes. I picked it up last week. Pretty?"

"Indecent. I didn't know it was a formal thing tonight."

"Not really. Optional anyway. Some of us decided to dress, that's all." She looked at him in the mirror and said, "I really don't care if you want to wear that suit."

Wordlessly he turned and went back to the closet to find his dinner jacket and black trousers. How easy it would be, a flick of a chain latch, and she'd be stripped to her hips. Was she counting on someone's noticing that? Evers maybe? Or Olivetti? Olivetti? What had he said? Something about women who wore red in public. Like passing out a dance card and pencil, the promise implicit in the gesture?

"Slut!" he said, through teeth so tightly pressed together that his jaws ached.

"What? I'm sorry."

He looked up. The woman in the bus station was watching him across the aisle. She still looked quite cold.

"I am sorry," she said softly. "I thought you spoke."

"No." He stuffed the policy back in his case and fastened it. "Are you warm enough?"

"Not really. The ticket agent wasn't kidding when he said the thermostat lies. According to it, it's seventy-four in here."

Crane got up and looked at the thermostat. The adjustment control was gone. The station was abysmally cold. He walked back and forth for a few moments, then paused at the window. The white world, ebbing and growing, changing, changeless. "If I had a cup or something, I could bring in some snow and chill the thermostat. That might make the heat kick on."

"Maybe in the rest room. . . ." He heard her move across the floor, but he didn't turn to look. There was a pink glow now in the whiteness, like a fire in the distance, all but obscured by the intervening clouds of snow. He watched as it grew brighter, darker, almost red; then it went out. The woman returned and stood at his side.

"No cups, but I folded paper towels to make a funnel thing. Will it do?"

He took the funnel. It was sturdy enough, three thicknesses of brown, unabsorbent toweling. "Probably better than a cup," he said. "Best stand behind the door. Every time it opens, that blizzard comes right on in."

She nodded and moved away. When he opened the door the wind hit him hard, almost knocking him back into the room, wrenching the door from his hand. It swung wide open and hit the woman. Distantly he heard her gasp of surprise and pain. He reached out and scooped up the funnel full of snow and then pushed the door closed again. He was covered with snow. Breathless, he leaned against the wall. "Are you all right?" he asked after a few moments.

She was holding her left shoulder. "Yes. It caught me by surprise. No harm done. Did you get enough snow?"

He held up the funnel for her to see and then pushed himself away from the wall. Again he had the impression that there was no right side up in the small station. He held the back of one of the benches and moved along it. "The wind took my breath away," he said.

"Or the intense cold. I think I read that breathing in the cold causes as many heart attacks as overexertion."

"Well, it's cold enough out there. About zero by now, I guess." He scooped out some of the snow and held it against the thermostat. "The furnace must be behind this wall, or under this area. Feel how warm it is."

She put her hand on the wall and nodded. "Maybe we can fasten the cup of snow up next to the thermostat." She looked around and then went to the bulletin board. She removed several of the notices and schedules there and brought him the thumbtacks. Crane spilled a little snow getting the tacks into the paper towel and then into the wall. In a few minutes there was a rumble as the furnace came on and almost immediately the station began to feel slightly warmer. Presently the woman took off her coat.

"Success," she said, smiling.

"I was beginning to think it had been a mistake after all, not going to the diner."

"So was I."

"I think they are trying to get the snowplows going. I saw a red light a couple of minutes ago. It went out again, but at least someone's trying."

She didn't reply, and after a moment he said, "I'm glad you don't smoke. I gave it up a few months ago, and it would drive me mad to have to smell it through a night like this. Probably I'd go back to them."

"I have some," she said. "I even smoke once in a while. If you decide that you do want them. . . ."

"No. No. I wasn't hinting."

"I just wish the lights were better in here. I could get in a whole night's work. I often work at night."

"So do I, but you'd put your eyes out. What—"

"That's all right. What kind of work do I do? An illustrator for Slocum House Catalogue Company. Not very exciting, I'm afraid."

"Oh, you're an artist."

"No. Illustrator. I wanted to become an artist, but . . . things didn't work out that way."

"I'd call you an artist. Maybe because I'm in awe of anyone who can draw, or paint, or do things like that. You're all artists to me."

She shrugged. "And you're an insurance salesman." He stiffened and she got up, saying, "I saw the policy you were looking over, and the briefcase stuffed full of policies and company pamphlets and such. I knew an insurance salesman once."

He realized that he had been about to ask where she was going, and he clamped his jaw again and turned so that he wouldn't watch her go into the ladies' room.

He went to the window. The wind was still at gale force, but so silent. With the door closed, the station seemed far removed from the storm, and looking at it was like watching something wholly unreal, manufactured to amuse him perhaps. There were storm windows, and the building was very sturdy and probably very well insulated. Now, with the furnace working, it was snug and secure. He cupped his hands about his eyes, trying to see past the reflections in the window, but there was nothing. Snow, a drift up to the sill now, and the wind-driven snow that was like a sheer curtain being waved from above, touching the windows, fluttering back, touching again, hiding everything behind it.

She was taking a long time. He should have gone when she left. Now he had the awkward moment to face, of excusing himself or not, of timing it so that she wouldn't think he was leaving deliberately in order to dodge something that one or the other said or hinted. She had done it so easily and naturally. He envied people like her. Always so sure of themselves.

"Which face are you wearing tonight, Randy?" Mary Louise reached across the table and touched his cheek, then shook her head. "I can't always tell. When you're the successful salesman, you are so assured, so poised, charming, voluble even."

"And the other times? What am I these times?"

"Afraid."

Drawing back from her hand, tight and self-contained again, watchful, he said, "Isn't it lucky that I can keep the two separated then? How successful a salesman would I be if I put on the wrong face when I went to work?"

"I wonder if mixing it up a little might not be good for you. So you wouldn't sell a million dollars' worth of insurance a year, but you'd be a little happier when you're not working."

"Like you?"

"Not like me, God forbid. But at least I haven't given up looking for something. And you have."

"Yeah. You're looking. In a bottle. In someone else's bed. In buying sprees."

"*C'est la vie.* You can always buzz off, you know."

"And add alimony to my other headaches? No thanks."

Smiling at him, sipping an old-fashioned, infinitely wise and infinitely evil. Were wise women always evil? "My poor Randy. My poor darling. You thought I was everything you were not, and instead you find that I am stamped from the same mold. Number XLM 119543872—afraid of life, only not quite afraid of death. Someone let up on the pressure there. Hardly an indentation even. So I can lose myself and you can't. A pity, my darling Randy. If we could lose ourselves together, what might we be able to find? We are so good together, you know. Sex with you is still the best of all. I try harder and harder to make you let go all the way. I read manuals and take personalized lessons, all for your sake, darling. All for you. And it does no good. You are my only challenge, you see."

"Stop it! Are you crazy?"

"Ah. Now I know who you are tonight. There you are. Tight mouth, frowning forehead full of lines, narrowed eyes. You are not so handsome with this face on, you know. Why don't you look at me, Randy?" Her hands across the table again, touching his cheeks, a finger trailing across his lips, a caress or mockery. "You never look at me, you know. You never look at me at all."

He leaned his forehead against the window, and the chill roused him. Where was the woman? He looked at his watch and realized that she had been gone only a few minutes, not the half hour or longer that he had thought. Was the whole night going to be like that? Minutes dragging by like hours? Time distorted until a lifetime could be spent in waiting for one dawn?

He went to the men's room. When he returned, she was sitting in her own place once more, her coat thrown over her shoulders, a sketch pad in her lap.

"Are you cold again?" He felt almost frozen. There was no heat in the men's room.

"Not really. Moving about chilled me. There's a puddle under the funnel, and the snow is gone, but heat is still coming from the radiator."

"I'll have to refill it every half hour or so, I guess."

"The driver said it's supposed to go to ten or fifteen below tonight."

Crane shrugged. "After it gets this low, I don't care how much farther it drops. As long as I don't have to be out in it."

She turned her attention to her pad and began to make strong lines. He couldn't tell what she was drawing, only that she didn't hesitate, but drew surely, confidently. He opened his briefcase and got out his schedule book. It was no use, he couldn't read the small print in the poor lighting of the station. He rummaged for something that he would be able to concentrate on. He was grateful when she spoke again:

"It was so stupid to start out tonight. I could have waited until tomorrow. I'm not bound by a time clock or anything."

"That's just what I was thinking. I was afraid of being snowed in for several days. We were at Sky Mount Ski Lodge, and everyone else was cheering the storm's approach. Do you ski?"

"Some, not very well. The cold takes my breath away, hitting me in the face like that."

He stared at her for a moment, opened his mouth to agree, then closed it again. It was as if she was anticipating what he was going to say.

"Don't be so silly, Randy. All you have to do is wear the muffler around your mouth and nose. And the goggles on your eyes. Nothing is exposed then. You're just too lazy to ski."

"Okay, lazy. I know this, I'm bored to death here. I haven't been warm since we left the apartment, and my legs ache. That was a nasty fall I had this morning. I'm sore. I have a headache from the glare of the snow, and I think it's asinine to freeze for two hours in order to slide down a mountain a couple of times. I'm going back to the city."

"But our reservation is through Saturday night. Paid in advance."

"Stay. Be my guest. Have yourself a ball. You and McCone make a good pair, and his wife seems content to sit on the sidelines and watch you. Did you really think that anemic blonde would appeal to me? Did you think we'd be too busy together to notice what you were up to?"

"Tracy? To tell the truth I hadn't given her a thought. I didn't know she didn't ski until this afternoon. I don't know why Mac brought her here. Any more than I know why you came along."

"Come on home with me. Let's pack up and leave before the

storm begins. We can stop at that nice old antique inn on the way home, where they always have pheasant pie. Remember?"

"Darling, I came to ski. You will leave the car here, won't you? I'll need it to get the skis back home, and our gear. Isn't there a bus or something?"

"Mary Louise, this morning on the slope, didn't you really see me? You know, when your ski pole got away from you."

"What in the world are you talking about? You were behind me. How could I have seen you? I didn't even know you had started down."

"Okay. Forget it. I'll give you a call when I get to the apartment."

"Yes, do. You can leave a message at the desk if I don't answer."

The woman held up her sketch and narrowed her eyes. She ripped out the page and crumpled it, tossed it into the wastecan.

"I think I'm too tired after all."

"It's getting cold in here again. Your hands are probably too cold." He got up and took the funnel from the wall. "I'll get more snow and see if we can't get the furnace going again."

"You should put something over your face, so the cold air won't be such a shock. Don't you have a muffler?"

He stopped. He had crushed the funnel, he realized, and he tried to smooth it again without letting her see what he had done. He decided that it would do, and opened the door. A drift had formed, and a foot of snow fell into the station. The wind was colder, sharper, almost deliberately cutting. He was blinded by the wind and the snow that was driven into his face. He filled the funnel and tried to close the door again, but the drift was in the way. He pushed, trying to use the door as a snowplow. More snow was being blown in, and finally he had to use his hands, push the snow out of the way, not outside, but to one side of the door. At last he had it clear enough and he slammed the door, more winded this time than before. His throat felt raw, and he felt a constriction about his chest.

"It's getting worse all the time. I couldn't even see the bus, nothing but a mountain of snow."

"Ground blizzard, I suspect. When it blows like this you can't tell how much of it is new snow and how much is just fallen snow being blown about. The drifts will be tremendous tomorrow." She smiled. "I remember how we loved it when this happened when we were kids. The drifts are exciting, so pure, so high. Sometimes they glaze over and you can play Glass Mountain. I used to be the princess."

Crane was shivering again. He forced his hands to be steady as he pushed the thumbtacks into the funnel to hold it in place next to the thermostat. He had to clear his throat before he could speak. "Did the prince ever reach you?"

"No. Eventually I just slid back down and went home."

"Where? Where did you live?"

"Outside Chicago, near the lake."

He spun around. "Who are you?" He grabbed the back of a bench and clutched it hard. She stared at him. He had screamed at her, and he didn't know why. "I'm sorry," he said. "You keep saying things that I'm thinking. I was thinking of that game, of how I never could make it to the top."

"Near Lake Michigan?"

"On the shores almost."

She nodded.

"I guess all kids play games like that in the snow," he said. "Strange that we should have come from the same general area. Did your milk freeze on the back steps, stick up out of the bottle, with the cap at an angle?"

"Yes. And those awful cloakrooms at school, where you had to strip off snowsuits and boots, and step in icy water before you could get your indoors shoes on."

"And sloshing through the thaws, wet every damn day. I was wet more than I was dry all through grade school."

"We all were," she said, smiling faintly, looking past him.

He almost laughed in his relief. He went to the radiator and put his hands out over it, his back to her. Similar backgrounds, that's all, he said to himself, framing the words carefully. Nothing strange. Nothing eerie. She was just a plain woman who came from the same state, probably the same county that he came from. They might have gone to the same schools, and he would not have noticed her. She was too common, too nondescript to have noticed at the time. And he had been a quiet boy, not particularly noteworthy himself. No sports besides the required ones. No clubs. A few friends, but even there, below average, because they had lived in an area too far removed from most of the kids who went to his school.

"It's only two. Seems like it ought to be morning already, doesn't it." She was moving about and he turned to see what she was doing. She had gone behind the counter, where the ticket agent had said there was a telephone. "A foam cushion," she said, holding it up. "I feel like one of the Swiss Family Robinson, salvaging what might be useful."

"Too bad there isn't some coffee under there."

"Wish you were in the diner?"

"No. That bitch probably has them all at each other's throats by now, as it is."

"That girl? The one who was so afraid?"

He laughed harshly and sat down. "Girl!"

"No more than twenty, if that much."

He laughed again and shook his head.

"Describe her to me," the woman said. She left the counter and sat down on the bench opposite him, still carrying the foam cushion. It had a black plastic cover, gray foam bulged from a crack. It was disgusting.

Crane said, "The broad was in her late twenties, or possibly thirties—"

"Eighteen to twenty."

"She had a pound of makeup on, nails like a cat."

"Fake nails, chapped hands, calluses. Ten-cent store makeup."

"She had expensive perfume, and a beaver coat. I think beaver."

She laughed gently. "Drugstore spray cologne. Macy's Basement fake fur, about fifty-nine to sixty-five dollars, unless she hit a sale."

"And the kid gloves, and the high patent-leather boots?"

"Vinyl, both of them." She looked at him for an uncomfortable minute, then examined the pillow she had found. "On second thought, I'm not sure that I would want to rest my head on this. It's a little bit disgusting, isn't it?"

"Why did you want me to describe that woman? You have your opinion of what she is; I have mine. There's no way to prove either of our cases without having her before us."

"I don't need to prove anything. I don't care if you think you're right and I'm wrong. I felt very sorry for the girl. I noticed her."

"I noticed her, too."

"What color was her hair, her eyes? How about her mouth, big, small, full? And her nose? Straight, snub, broad?"

He regarded her bitterly for a moment, then shrugged and turned toward the window. He didn't speak.

"You can't describe what she really was like because you didn't see her. You saw the package and made up your mind about the contents. Believe me, she was terrified of the storm, of those men, everything. She needed the security of the driver and people. What about me? Can you describe me?"

He looked, but she was holding the pillow between them and he could see only her hands, long, pale, slender fingers, no rings.

"This is ridiculous," he said after a second. "I have one of those reputations for names and faces. You know, never forget a name, always know the names of the kids, the wife, occupation, and so on."

"Not this side of you. This side refuses to see anyone at all. I wonder why."

"What face are you wearing tonight, Randy?" Mary Louise

touching him. "Do you see me? Why don't you look at me?"

Wind whistling past his ears, not really cold yet, not when he was standing still anyway, with the sun warm on him. But racing down the slope, trees to his right, the precipice to his left, the wind was icy. Mary Louise a red streak ahead of him, and somewhere behind him the navy and white blur that was McCone. Holding his own between them. The curve of the trail ahead, the thrill of the downward plummet, and suddenly the openmouthed face of his wife, silent scream, and in the same instant, the ski pole against his legs, tripping him up, the more exciting plunge downward, face in the snow, blinded, over and over, skis gone now, trying to grasp the snow, trying to stop the tumbling, over and over in the snow.

Had his wife tried to kill him?

"Are you all right, Mr. Crane?"

"Yes, of course. Let me describe the last man I sold insurance to, a week ago. Twenty-four, six feet one inch, a tiny, almost invisible scar over his right eyebrow, crinkle lines about his eyes, because he's an outdoor type, very tanned and muscular. He's a professional baseball player, incidentally. His left hand has larger knuckles than the right . . ."

The woman was not listening. She had crossed the station and was standing at the window, trying to see out. "Computer talk," she said. "A meaningless rundown of facts. So he bought a policy for one hundred thousand dollars, straight life, and from now on you won't have to deal with him, be concerned with him at all."

"Why did you say one hundred thousand dollars?"

"No reason. I don't know, obviously."

He chewed his lip and watched her. "Any change out there?"

"Worse, if anything. I don't think you'll be able to use this door at all now. You'd never get it closed. It's half covered with a drift."

"There must be a window or another door that isn't drifted over."

"Storm windows. Maybe there's a back door, but I bet it opens to the office, and the ticket agent locked that."

Crane looked at the windows and found that she was right. The storm windows couldn't be opened from inside. And there wasn't another outside door. The men's room was like a freezer now. He tried to run the water, thinking that possibly cold water would work on the thermostat as well as snow, but nothing came out. The pipes must have frozen. As he started to close the door, he saw a small block-printed sign: "Don't close door all the way, no heat in here, water will freeze up." The toweling wouldn't hold water anyway.

He left the door open a crack and rejoined the woman near the window. "It's got to be this door," he said. "I guess I could open it an inch or two, let that much of the drift fall inside and use it."

"Maybe. But you'll have to be careful."

"Right out of Jack London," he said. "It's seventy-two on the thermometer. How do you feel?"

"Coolish, not bad."

"Okay, we'll wait awhile. Maybe the wind will let up."

He stared at the puddle under the thermostat, and at the other larger one across the room near the door, where the snowdrift had entered the room the last time. The drift had been only a foot high then, and now it was three or four feet. Could he move that much snow without anything to work with, if it came inside?

He shouldn't have started back to town. She had goaded him into it, of course. Had she suspected that he would get stranded somewhere, maybe freeze to death?

"Why don't you come right out and say what you're thinking?" Red pants, red ski jacket, cheeks almost as red.

"I'm not thinking anything. It was an accident."

"You're a liar, Randy! You think I guessed you were there, that I let go hoping to make you fall. Isn't that what you think? Isn't it?"

He shook his head hard. She hadn't said any of that. He hadn't thought of it then. Only now, here, stranded with this half-mad woman. Half-mad? He looked at her and quickly averted his gaze. Why had that thought come to him? She was odd, certainly, probably very lonely, shy. But half-mad?

Why did she watch him so? As if aware of his thoughts, she turned her back and walked to the ladies' room. He had to go too, but he remembered the frozen pipes in the men's room. Maybe she'd fall asleep eventually and he'd be able to slip into her rest room. If not, then he'd wait until morning. Maybe this night had come about in order to give him time to think about him and Mary Louise, to really think it through all the way and come to a decision.

He had met her when he was stationed in Washington, after the Korean War. He had been a captain, assigned to Army Intelligence. She had worked as a private secretary to Senator Robertson of New York. So he had done all right without her up to then. She had introduced him to the president of the company that he worked for now. Knowing that he wanted to become a writer, she had almost forced him into insurance. Fine. It was the right choice. He had told her so a thousand times. But how he had succeeded was still a puzzle to him. He never had tested well in salesmanship on aptitude tests. Too introverted and shy.

"You make other people feel stupid, frankly," she had said once. "You are so tight and so sure of yourself that you don't allow anyone else to have an opinion at all. It's not empathy, like it is with so many good salesmen. It's a kind of sadistic force that you apply."

"Oh, stop it. You're talking nonsense."

"You treat each client like an extension of the policy that you intend to sell to him. Not like a person, but the human counterpart of the slick paper with the clauses and small print. You show the same respect and liking for them as for the policies. They go together. You believe it and make them believe it.

Numbers, that's what they are to you. Policy numbers."

"Why do you hang around if you find me so cold and calculating?"

"Oh, it's a game that I play. I know there's a room somewhere where you've locked up part of yourself, and I keep searching for it. Someday I'll find it and open it just a crack, and then I'll run. Because if it ever opens, even a little, everything will come tumbling out and you won't be able to stop any of it. How you'll bleed then, bleed and bleed, and cry and moan. I couldn't stand that. And I can't stand for it not to be so."

Crane put his head down in his hands and rubbed his eyes hard. Without affect, that was the term that she used. Modern man without affect. Schizoid personality. But he also had a nearly split personality. The doctor had told him so. In the six sessions that he had gone to he had learned much of the jargon, and then he had broken it off. Split personality. Schizoid tendencies. Without affect. All to keep himself safe. It seemed to him to be real madness to take away any of the safeties he had painstakingly built, and he had quit the sessions.

And now this strange woman that he was locked up with was warning him not to open the door a crack. He rubbed his eyes harder until there was solid pain there. He had to touch her. The ticket agent had seen her, too, though. He had been concerned about leaving her alone with a strange man all night. So transparently worried about her, worried about Crane. Fishing for his name. He could have told the fool anything. He couldn't remember his face at all, only his clothes.

All right, the woman was real, but strange. She had an uncanny way of anticipating what he was thinking, what he was going to say, what he feared. Maybe these were her fears, too.

She came back into the waiting room. She was wearing her black coat buttoned to her neck, her hands in the pockets. She didn't mention the cold.

Soon he would have to get more snow, trick the fool thermostat into turning on the furnace. Soon. A maniac must have put it on that wall, the only warm wall in the building. A penny-pinching maniac.

"If you decide to try to get more snow, maybe I should hold the door while you scoop it up," she said, after a long silence. The cold had made her face look pinched, and Crane was shivering under his overcoat.

"Can you hold it?" he asked. "There's a lot of pressure behind that door."

She nodded.

"Okay. I'll take the wastecan and get as much as I can. It'll keep in the men's room. There's no heat in there."

She held the doorknob until he was ready, and when he nodded, she turned it and, bracing the door with her shoulder, let it open several inches. The wind pushed, and the snow spilled through. It was over their heads now, and it came in the entire height of the door. She gave ground and the door was open five or six inches. Crane pulled the snow inside, using both hands, clawing at it. The Augean stable, he thought bitterly, and then joined her behind the door, trying to push it closed again. At least no blast of air had come inside this time. The door was packing the snow, and the inner surface of it was thawing slightly, only to refreeze under the pressure and the cold from the other side. Push, Crane thought at her. Push, you devil. You witch.

Slowly it began to move, scrunching snow. They weren't going to get it closed all the way. They stopped pushing to rest. He was panting hard, and she put her head against the door. After a moment he said, "Do you think you could move one of the benches over here?"

She nodded. He braced himself against the door and was surprised at the increase in the pressure when she left. He heard her wrestling with the bench, but he couldn't turn to see. The snow was gaining again. His feet were slipping on the floor, wet now where some of the snow had melted and was running across the room. He saw the bench from the corner of his eye,

and he turned to watch her progress with it. She was pushing
it toward him, the back to the wall; the back was too high. It
would have to be tilted to go under the doorknob. It was a heavy
oak bench. If they could maneuver it in place, it would hold.

For fifteen minutes they worked, grunting, saying nothing,
trying to hold the door closed and get the bench under the knob
without losing any more ground. Finally it was done. The door
was open six inches, white packed snow the entire height of it.

Crane fell onto a bench and stared at the open door, not able
to say anything. The woman seemed equally exhausted. At the
top of the door, the snow suddenly fell forward, into the station,
sifting at first, then falling in a stream. Icy wind followed the
snow into the room, and now that the top of the column of snow
had been lost, the wind continued to pour into the station,
whistling shrilly.

"Well, we know now that the drift isn't really to the top of the
building," the woman said wearily. She was staring at the opening.

"My words, almost exactly," Crane said. She always said what
he planned to say. He waited.

"We'll have to close it at the top somehow."

He nodded. "In a minute. In a minute."

The cold increased and he knew that he should get busy and
try to close the opening, but he felt too numb to cope with it.
The furnace couldn't keep up with the draft of below-zero air.
His hands were aching with cold, and his toes hurt with a stab-
bing intensity. Only his mind felt pleasantly numb and he didn't
want to think about the problem of closing up the hole.

"You're not falling asleep, are you?"

"For God's sake!" He jerked straight up on the bench and
gave her a mean look, a guilty look. "Just shut up and let me try
to think, will you?"

"Sorry." She got up and began to pace briskly, hugging her
hands to her body. "I'll look around, see if I can find anything
that would fit. I simply can't sit still, I'm so cold."

He stared at the hole. There had to be something that would fit over it, stay in place, keep out the wind. He narrowed his eyes, staring, and he saw the wind-driven snow as a liquid running into the station from above, swirling about, only fractionally heavier than the medium that it met on the inside. One continuum, starting in the farthest blackest vacuum of space, taking on form as it reached the highest atmospheric molecules, becoming denser as it neared Earth, almost solid here, but not yet. Not yet. The hole extended to that unimaginable distance where it all began, and the chill spilled down, down, searching for him, wafting about here, searching for him, wanting only to find him, willing then to stop the ceaseless whirl. Coat him, claim him. The woman belonged to the coldness that came from the black of space. He remembered her now.

Korea. The woman. The village. Waiting for the signal. Colder than the station even, snow, flintlike ground, striking sparks from nails in boots, sparks without warmth. If they could fire the village, they would get warm, have food, sleep that night. Harrison, wounded, frozen where he fell. Lorenz, frostbitten; Jakobs, snow-blind. Crane, too tired to think, too hungry to think, too cold to think. "Fire the village." The woman, out of nowhere, urging him back, back up the mountain to the bunkers that were half filled with ice, mines laid now between the bunkers and the valley. Ordering the woman into the village at gunpoint. Spark from his muzzle. Blessed fire and warmth. But a touch of ice behind the eyes, ice that didn't let him weep when Lorenz died, or when Jakobs, blinded, wandered out and twitched and jerked and pitched over a cliff under a fusillade of bullets. The snow queen, he thought. She's the snow queen, and she touched my eyes with ice.

"Mr. Crane, please wake up. Please!"

He jumped to his feet reaching for his carbine, and only when his hands closed on air did he remember where he was.

"Mr. Crane, I think I know what we can use to close up the hole. Let me show you."

She pulled at his arm and he followed her. She led him into the ladies' room. At the door he tried to pull back, but she tugged. "Look, stacks of paper towels, all folded together. They would be about the right size, wouldn't they? If we wet them, a block of them, and if we can get them up to the hole, they would freeze in place, and the drift could pile up against them and stop blowing into the station. Wouldn't it work?"

She was separating the opened package into thirds, her hands busy, her eyes downcast, not seeing him at all. Crane, slightly to one side of her, a step behind, stared at the double image in the mirror. He continued to watch the mirror as his hands reached out for her and closed about her throat. There was no struggle. She simply closed her eyes and became very limp, and he let her fall. Then he took the wad of towels and held it under the water for a few moments and returned to the waiting room with it. He had to clear snow from the approach to the door, and then he had to move the bench that was holding the door, carefully, not letting it become dislodged. He dragged a second bench to the door and climbed on it and pushed the wet wad of towels into the opening. He held it several minutes, until he could feel the freezing paper start to stiffen beneath his fingers. He climbed down.

"That should do it," the woman said.

"But you're dead."

Mary Louise threw the sugar bowl at him, trailing a line of sugar across the room.

He smiled. "Wishful thinking," he/she said.

"You're dead inside. You're shriveled up and dried up and rotting inside. When did you last feel anything? My God! You can't create anything, you are afraid of creating anything, even our child!"

"I don't believe it was our child."

"You don't dare believe it. Or admit that you know it was."

He slapped her. The only time that he ever hit her. And her so pale from the operation, so weak from the loss of blood. The slap meant nothing to him, his hand meeting her cheek, leaving a red print there.

"Murderer!"

"You crazy bitch! You're the one who had the abortion! You wanted it!"

"I didn't. I didn't know what I wanted. I was terrified. You made the arrangements, got the doctor, took me, arranged everything, waited in the other room writing policies. Murderer."

"Murderer," the woman said.

He shook his head. "You'd better go back to the ladies' room and stay there. I don't want to hurt you."

"Murderer."

He took a step toward her. He swung around abruptly and almost ran to the far side of the station, pressing his forehead hard on the window.

"We can't stop it now," the woman said, following him. "You can't close the door again now. I'm here. You finally saw me. Really saw me. I'm real now. I won't be banished again. I'm stronger than you are. You've killed off bits and pieces of yourself until there's nothing left to fight with. You can't send me away again."

Crane pushed himself away from the glass and made a half-hearted attempt to hit her with his fist. He missed and fell against the bench holding the door. He heard the woman's low laugh. All for nothing. All for nothing. The bench slid out from under his hand, and the drift pushed into the room like an avalanche. He pulled himself free and tried to brush the snow off his clothes.

"We'll both freeze now," he said, not caring any longer.

The woman came to his side and touched his cheek with her fingers; they were strangely warm. "Relax now, Crane. Just relax."

She led him to a bench where he sat down resignedly. "Will you at least tell me who you are?" he said.

"You know. You've always known."

He shook his head. One last attempt, he thought. He had to make that one last effort to get rid of her, the woman whose face was so like his own. "You don't even exist," he said harshly, not opening his eyes. "I imagined you here because I was afraid of being alone all night. I created you. *I created you.*"

He stood up. "You hear that, Mary Louise! Did you hear that? I created something. Something so real that it wants to kill me."

"Look at me, Crane. Look at me. Turn your head and look. Look with me, Crane. Let me show you. Let me show you what I see. . . ."

He was shaking again, chilled through, shaking so hard that his muscles were sore. Slowly, inevitably he turned his head and saw the man half-standing, half-crouching, holding the bench with both hands. The man had gray skin, and his eyes were mad with terror.

"Let go, Crane. Look at him and let go. He doesn't deserve anything from us ever again." Crane watched the man clutch his chest, heard him moaning for Mary Louise to come help him, watched him fall to the floor.

She heard the men working at the drift, and she opened the office door to wait for them. They finally got through and the ticket agent squirmed through the opening they had made.

"Miss! Miss? Are you all right?"

"Yes. I broke into the office, though."

"My God, I thought . . . When we saw that the door had given under the drift, and you in here . . . alo—" The ticket agent blinked rapidly several times.

"I was perfectly all right. When I saw that the door wasn't going to hold, I broke open the inner office and came in here with my sketch book and pencils. I've had a very productive night, really. But I could use some coffee now."

They took her to the diner in a police car, and while she waited for her breakfast order, she went to the rest room and washed her face and combed her hair. She stared at herself in the mirror appraisingly. "Happy birthday," she said softly then.

"Your birthday?" asked the girl who had chosen to wait the night out in the diner. "You were awfully brave to stay alone in the station. I couldn't have done that. You really an artist?"

"Yes, really. And last night I had a lot of work to get done. A lot of work and not much time."

Planet Story

THERE IS NOTHING to fear on this planet.

The planet is represented in our records by a series of numbers and letters, each conveying information: distance from its sun, mass, period of rotation, presence or absence of a moon, or moons. The seedling colony that will arrive some day will name the planet.

We are twenty-seven men and women planet-side, and three more who remain on the orbiting ship—minimum age twenty-five, maximum age fifty. This is the fourth Earth year of a seven-year contract. There were twenty-eight of us planet-side but Ito went mad and committed suicide twenty days ago, on the seventh day here.

There is abundant life here, a full spectrum from viruses to high order mammals. The animals do not fear us. We walk among them freely. Each is conditioned to fear its predator and to search out its prey. Nowhere in that scheme does man fit in.

The sun is a bright yellow glow in the clouds; it moves like a searchlight in fog to complete its trip in thirty-four hours. The planet's month is thirty-seven days. On the thirty-eighth day we shall leave. We shall take nothing with us except data, facts—a paragraph in the catalogue of worlds. With our lives we are

75

buying insurance for the family of Earthmen.

Olga watches me with brooding eyes, for twice I have spurned her, while I in turn watch Haarlem, a distant figure at the moment, operating his core drill with such precision and concentration it is as if he has become an extension of the mechanism he uses. I wonder at the affinity that sometimes exists between man and his machinery, an affinity that seems reciprocal in that now the will of the human rules, and again he is ruled by the demands of his tool. I concentrate on Olga and Haarlem and my abstract thoughts because here within reach of the ship, in sight of my friends and co-workers, I am afraid.

My buzzer sounds and I turn it off and go back to the ship, the end of my duty break. Since Ito's death we have taken turns at the computer, coding the data, transmitting everything to our orbiting ship. Should Haarlem die, another would operate his core drill, complete his geological survey; should I die, another would don my doctor's garb and check temperatures, administer to the ill and injured. I wait for my signal to activate the steps and the airlock door to the decontamination chamber and as I wait I watch Haarlem, a distant figure. I am eager to be inside, my suit off, breathing the air of the ship, not that from my oxypack, and I want to whirl about, to find whatever it is making my heart beat too fast.

On this gentle continent, on this benign planet where there is no menace to mankind in the air, on the ground, beneath the ground, no menace of any kind, I am afraid. We all are afraid. No one speaks of his fear because there is nothing to allude to as a possible source. No sighing wind in the trees, no alien ghosts among ruins, no psychic call from a gloomy wood. Nothing. A broad plain of low vegetation; animals grazing; a hazy sky; a flock of small, furry, flying animals that appear soft and pettable; an iridescent gauzy wing of an insect that hovers, then darts away, insect-like.

There are no ruins on this planet. No artifacts. No intelligent

life has ever walked here until now. There is the plain that
stretches to the horizon to the east, and the hills rounded with
age and covered with trees spaced as if planned, park-like,
garden-like. Elvil assures us there is no plan, this is how trees
grow if left alone. There are the flowers that grow at the junc-
tion of the forest and plain: bushes with blue flowers, carpeting
plants with yellow masses of blooms, vines that curl and twist
their way up the trees that edge the forest. Red flowers hang
downward, with long slender stamens that sway with the wind,
like dancers in yellow tights against a scarlet velvet backdrop.
The flowers are the buffer zone between forest and plain, a
living flag of truce, promising no encroachment on the part of
either for ground already held by the other.

The steps descend and I climb upward and turn momentar-
ily, to see Olga's face lifted, as she watches me with brooding
eyes. I enter the chamber where a spray cleanses my suit, and
lights dry it and finish the process. I discard the garment and
step naked into the shower and remain under the warm water
for the alloted time, wishing it were longer, and, still naked, go
into the dressing room where Derek is preparing to go outside.
Elvil is assisting him.

I watch him dress and realize, belatedly, he is dressing for a
trip in one of the flyers. Our ships are like Chinese puzzle boxes:
Inside each there is a smaller one, which in turn contains another even smaller. We have three flyers on the landing ship,
each large enough for six or eight people. Two of them are with
the ocean party, and now Derek plans to use the third. He is
pulling on his heavier suit, his gloves are at his belt.

"Where are you going?"

"To the ocean group. Jeanne is missing."

I feel a lurch in my stomach. Jeanne? She is tall and has hair
the color of sun on pale sand, blindingly bright, with dark
streaks. Her skin is baby smooth and there is a joy in her that
makes her a favorite of everyone.

"They need a third car for the search," Derek says, and now

he is ready. Elvil double-checks him and he enters the decontamination chamber.

"They'll find her," Elvil says then, his hand heavy and cold on
my bare shoulder. I nod and clasp his hand briefly.

While the ship is on the ground the seats for thirty become
narrow beds, each with a screen that can be closed. When I am
relieved at the computer I find Olga waiting for me in my tiny
area of privacy.

"Please," she says, "don't make me leave. I only want to talk."

It is not yet dark outside; my mind is on the search that is
continuing along the ocean's edge. But I am very tired. I sit by
Olga and draw her close and hold her. She is trembling.

"I am so afraid," she whispers. "I keep looking around to see
what's there, and there's nothing. And that makes it worse."
Her trembling increases and I lie down with her and stroke her
and think of the search.

Olga is beautiful in a broad-hipped, large-breasted way that
is pure sensuality. Her responses to any touch are always sexual.
She apologizes for it often, but everyone understands her
needs, and few deny her the caresses she craves, the release she
must have. Her trembling now however is not caused by sexual
tension, but fear, and I don't know how to allay it.

We should have a meeting, an open session with everyone
present, and air our fears, I decide. After the search for Jeanne
is completed, I'll call a meeting here on the ship, another with
the shore party. Derek can preside there. He will know how to
conduct it, what to look for, how to force it along certain lines.

Olga moans and I turn my attention once more to her. She
.has forgotten her fear, at least for the moment. When I leave
her, she is sleeping peacefully.

The captain's office is next to my infirmary. He is a slender
man, with delicate hands, and he, like Haarlem, has an affinity
for his machines. Sometimes I feel he and the ship are one. His
face is deeply carved and often he is careless with his depilatory
cream and misses a fissure in which dark hairs grow luxuriantly,

until the next time he removes his beard. Those dark lines make his face look like a caricature. He is studying a monitor on his desk when I enter. It is the search area near the ocean. I read the moving lights as readily as he, but I ask anyway.

"Any news yet?"

"Nothing."

We continue to watch together for a few moments, and then I sit down opposite him and say, "She has done it deliberately then."

He nods. There are constant signals from the suits unless the wearer turns them off. Two buttons are involved requiring both hands to deactivate the signal system. It is an impossibility for it to happen accidentally.

"Like Ito," I say. Not like, but he knows what I mean. Ito hanged himself.

"I'm afraid so," he says. He looks at me, but doesn't turn off his monitor. "Have you any suggestions?"

"None. I'd like an open session, as soon as possible."

There is no immediate response. He must weigh the possible results: an increase of fear if it becomes acknowledged; a decrease; a cause identified; someone else being driven to suicide. There are ten days remaining to us on this planet. He says, "Today I found myself stopping to hear if there were footsteps behind me. I have been uneasy before, not like this though. I looked around before I could control myself."

"I know. It's getting worse." The kindest among us have become withdrawn, short tempered; the indifferent ones have become quarrelsome; the ones tending toward meanness in the best of times have become vicious. Always before, the ubiquitous dangers of unknown worlds have drawn us closer, but here, in the total absence of any threat, we are struggling to free ourselves from the mutual dependency that is as necessary to our success as the individual skills each brings to the service. I shrug. "I look, too," I say. "There's nothing."

He glances at the search monitor and says, "When do you want your session?"

"When we get up, before sunrise." It is a good time, when

defenses are down somewhat. Everyone will welcome a break
in the record-keeping chores that occupy us all in the hours
after we sleep and before sunrise. The nights are very long on
this planet with its thirty-four-hour day.

I rise to leave him and pause before stepping over the portal.
"I'm sorry about Jeanne, Wes." I know she was a favorite of his,
also. He has few he can turn to. Something keeps him aloof from
the rest of us, but he had Jeanne and now he won't have her.
I am sorry.

High above the atmosphere of this planet the orbiting ship is
studying the sun. Closer, spy satellites weave an invisible web
as they spin in their separate orbits, mapping the world, sensing
mineral deposits, ocean depths, volcanic regions. On the surface, our group, split into halves, makes a minute examination
of the soil, the air, the rivers and shores, the animal life. This
planet can withhold no secrets from our assault: the nitrogen
content of the soil, the bone composition of the animals, the
oxygen dissolved in the streams, the parts per million of spores,
bacteria, pollen in the air. Nothing will remain hidden. Our
preliminary reports prepared in the first three days indicated
there is nothing harmful to man on this planet.

The group that gathers for the open session knows all this. We
meet in the main room of the ship, where each of us has his own
seat-bed, with a screen to be closed at will. The seats are upright
now, the screens open.

We are a good group, I know. We can trust one another. We
know each has proven his bravery, his intelligence frequently
enough not to have it questioned. We are close enough emo-
tionally to be able to forego any preliminaries, intimate enough
to recognize any signs of hesitation or evasion.

"I would like to try to get a profile of whatever it is causing
our fears," I say. "Since there is nothing that anyone can see, or
detect with instruments, we might approach with the possibil-
ity that it is a projection. This is not a conclusion, merely a place
to start."

There are nods, and only Haarlem seems disapproving of this beginning. I call on him first. "Have you ever felt a comparable uneasiness that you couldn't rationalize?"

He shakes his head silently and I feel a flush of annoyance with him.

"Is there anyone who has felt a similar, baseless fear?"

"Once," Louenvelt says, "when I was a child, no more than four. I wakened with a feeling of great fear, afraid to move, unable to say why. Not the usual nightmare awakening, but similar to it. There had been an earthquake, quieted by the time I was thoroughly awake, but I didn't know that at the time." Louenvelt is our botanist, a quiet man who seldom participates in any group activity. I am grateful that he has started the session.

Sharkey is next to speak, and I know I will have to bear this, too. Sharkey is querulous: conversation with him is always one-sided and endless.

"On my first Contract," he says, with an air of settling in, "we were faced with these bear-like beings. Big. Big as grizzlies, that's why we called them bears, even though they . . ."

"But you knew what frightened you," I say firmly. "That isn't what we're after right now."

"Well, we knew those bears would tear us limb from limb, and they were smart, even if the computer did rate them non-intelligent. The dominant species: That always is a clue about . . ."

I depress the button of my recorder to underline what he has just said. He has given me something to think about after all. There is no dominant species on this planet.

Olga has stood up and there is excitement on her face. "You said it might be a projection," she says. "But what if it isn't? What if there are things that we can't detect simply because we've never had to detect them before?" Sharkey gives way to her amiably. He is used to being interrupted.

"What do you mean?" I ask. Olga is a zoologist, specializing in holographic scanning of animals. She can make replications of animals with her equipment, down to the nerve endings. With her holograms and a blood sample, a nail, hoof, or hair clipping, she can tell you what the animal customarily eats, its rate of growth, its life span.

"I mean that no matter how much information we have, we always have to add more with new facts. The computer can't be more intelligent than its programmers. We all know that. And if we are faced with something that no one has ever seen before, of course we haven't got that information in the computer. The sensors can't report what they haven't been programmed to sense, any more than a metal detector will indicate plastic." She sits down again with a smug air.

Haarlem says, "And the evidence of our eyes? And our ears? Are we to believe that we cannot hear or see because we have never experienced this before?" Haarlem is very dark, he keeps his head shaved, almost as if he wants to conceal nothing on the outside because he realizes that there are so many hidden places within. Olga has never repressed anything in her life. She is fair, open, quick to be wounded, quicker to heal. Haarlem bleeds internally for a long time.

"Yes, our eyes can deceive us," Olga says with some heat. "If a ghost walked in here, we would every one of us deny our eyes!"

Haarlem laughs and settles back to become a spectator once more. I study him briefly, wondering at his withdrawal, his almost sullen attitude that has kept me at a distance. I yearn for him, but in his present mood we only fight when we are together, and it is well that he rebuffs me, I decide. He is wiser in some matters than I am.

Julie tells of a time that she was overcome by fear in a deep wood in the Canadian Rockies, and someone else relates a similar feeling while at sea, standing alone in the stern of the ship. It goes on. Nearly everyone can remember such an incident, and when it is over, I wonder what we have accomplished, if we have accomplished anything. Perhaps we will all speak of it now when it occurs. Mel Souder, our meteorologist, will chart the times and check them against weather changes, wind shifts. I expect little to come of it.

My suit is lightweight and impermeable, my oxypack heavy on my back, an accustomed heaviness accepted as one accepts a gain in weight, or a swollen foot or hand. Awkward, but necessary. We do not breathe the air of the planets we discover. It is for the seedling colonists to take such risks, to adapt to the local conditions if necessary. We adapt to nothing but change.

This is how Jeanne walked away, I think, her footsteps clear in the sand, her tracing clear on the the recorder, until suddenly there was no longer any tracing, although the footprints continued up the beach another twenty or thirty meters, and then turned inland and were lost in the undergrowth of the tangled marsh trees and bushes.

There is a pale coloring in the sky now: first comes the lightening with no particular color, and then the clouds glow as if a fire is raging somewhere, obscured by smoke and fog that lets a crimson band appear, then a golden flare, then pale pink rolling clouds, and finally the yellow spot that is too bright to look at directly, but is not defined as a sun.

I walk along the edge of the flowers that divide the plain from the forest. The vegetation is grass-like, but not grass. It is broader leaved, pliable. It springs up behind me and shows no evidence of my passing. A swarm of jade insects rises and forms a column of life that hovers a moment, disperses, and settles once more, hidden again by the plants. There are birds here, song birds, birds of prey, shore birds. Every niche is filled from bacteria to mammals, but intelligence did not arise. Nor is there a dominant species.

I could go into the forest, walk for hours and never become lost. My belt has homing instruments that would guide me back to the ship. My oxypack has a signal to warn me when half of my supply of air is gone. And aboard ship, telltale tracings

would reveal my position at a glance to rescuers, should I fall
and be unable to continue.

I suppose I am mourning Jeanne, but more than that, I am
inviting the fear to come to me now. Always before I have been
where I could busy myself instantly, or return to the ship, or
seek out another and start a conversation designed to mask the
fear. It always comes to one who is alone, in a contemplative
mood possibly. Can the fear be courted? I don't know, but I will
know before I return to the ship.

The resilient blades under my feet make a faint sighing sound
as they straighten up. It is almost musical, a counterpoint to the
rhythm of my steps, so faint that only if I concentrate on it does
it become audible. I am becoming aware of other sounds. Something in the woods is padding along in the same direction that
I walk. I stop and search for it, but see nothing. When I move
again I listen for it and presently it is there. A small animal,
curious about me probably, not frightening. If a carnivore
should become confused and attack me, I would stop it long
before it could reach me. We are armed, and on many planets
the arms have been necessary, but not here. I wish to see the
small animal because, like it, I am curious.

From the giraffe to the platypus, from the elephant to the
shrew, the crocodile to the gibbon, such is the spread of life that
we have accepted on Earth, and wherever we have gone since
then, the range has been comparable. There are things that are
like, but not the same, and others that are unlike anything any
of us has seen before. The universal catalogue of animals would
need an entire planet to house its volumes. Perhaps Olga is
right, perhaps there are those things we cannot perceive because we are too inexperienced.

The small animal has become tired of its game, and walks out
from the brush to nibble yellow flowers. It is a pale gray quad-
ruped, short coarse hair, padded feet, tailless, and now it
evinces no interest in me at all. It is cat-like, but no one would
ever mistake it for a cat. An herbivorous cat.

The animals have struck a balance on this planet. Checks and balances work here. A steady population, enough food for all, no need for the genocidal competition of other worlds. This, I feel, is the key to the planet. I have stopped to observe the cat-like animal, and now I start to walk once more, and suddenly there it is.

There has been no change in anything as far as I can tell. No sound of parallel steps, no rustling in the grass. The wind hasn't changed. Nothing has changed, but I feel the first tendrils of fear raising the hairs of my arms, playing over my scalp. I study the woods while the fear grows. Then the plain. A small furry animal flies overhead, oblivious of me, intent on his own flight into the woods. Now I can feel my heart race and I begin to speak into my recorder, trying to put into words that which is only visceral and exists without symbols or signs that can truly define it. My physiological symptoms are not what my fear is. I describe them anyway. Now my hands are perspiring heavily and I begin to feel nausea rise and spread, weakening my legs, cramping my stomach. I am searching faster, looking for something, anything. Something to fight or run away from. And there is nothing. My heart is pounding hard and the urge to scream and run is very strong. The urge to run into the woods and hide myself among the trees is strong also, as is the urge to drop to the ground and draw myself up into as tight and hard a ball as possible and become invisible. Nothing in the overcast sky, nothing in the woods, nothing on the plain, nothing . . . From the ground then. Something coming up from the ground. I am running and sobbing into my recorder, running from the spot where it has to to be, and it runs with me.

I am in the woods and can't remember entering them, I remember telling myself I would not enter them. Now I can no longer see the ship in the distance and the fear is growing and pressing in on me, crushing me down into the ground. I think, if I vomit I might drown in it. The suits were not made for that contingency. I would have to take off the helmet, and expose myself to it even more.

If I turn off all my devices, then it won't be able to find me.

I can hide in the woods then. Even as the thought occurs to me
I start to scream. I fall to the ground and claw and scrabble at
it, and I scream and scream.

I begged them not to give me a sedative, but Wes counter-
manded me and administered it personally and I slept. Now it
is late afternoon and much of the morning is dream-like, but I
know this will pass as the sedative wears off. They think I am
mad, like Ito, like Jeanne probably was at the end. I am very
sore. I believe I fought them when they found me in the woods
clawing a hole in the ground, screaming.

I am in a restraining sheet and there is nothing I can do but
wait until someone comes to see about me. Not Sharkey, I hope.
But Wes is too considerate and wise to permit Sharkey access
to someone who cannot walk away.

It is Wes who looks in on me, and behind him I can see
Haarlem. "I'm all right," I say. "Pulse normal, no fever, calm.
You can release me, you know."

"How did you take your pulse?" Haarlem asks, not disbeliev-
ing, but interested.

"In the groin. I have to talk to you and this sheet makes it
damned difficult."

Wes releases the restraint and I sit up. Before I can start, he
says, "If you have found out anything at all, let's have it straight.
Now. The clouds have lifted and for the first time we have the
opportunity for aerial reconnaissance, and I want to go along."

The cloud cover of this planet is not thick, not like on Venus,
but since our arrival there has been a haze, there have been no
sharp features that were visible from the aircraft. Probably a
spring feature, the meteorologist said, that would not be a factor
throughout the rest of the year. With the lifting of the clouds
there would be sharp shadows, and clearly defined trees and
streams, and peaceful animals that would look with wonder on
the things in the sky.

Inside the Chinese puzzle box are other boxes, each smaller
than the last, and our innermost box is the one-man aircraft.

"You mustn't go," I say. "Don't let anyone go anywhere alone again."

The captain clears his throat and even opens his mouth but it is Haarlem who speaks first. "What happened to you?"

I tell them quickly, leaving out nothing. "I recorded all of it," I say. "Until I started to scream. I turned that off."

"You knew you were going to scream?" Wes asks with some surprise, or possibly disbelief.

"I had to. The adrenalin prepares one to fight, or to run. If he can do neither and sometimes even if he can, the excess adrenalin can change the chemistry of the brain and the person may go mad. Like Ito. Or lose consciousness. I chose to do neither. Screaming is another outlet, and I had to do something with my hands, or they would have clawed at the buttons of my controls. So I dug and screamed."

"And what have you proved?" Haarlem asks. He sounds angry now.

I continue to look at Wes. "It gets overwhelming if the person is alone, beyond the reach of others, or the ship. And there is no living thing present to account for it. Unlike other fear situations where the fear peaks and then subsides, this doesn't diminish, but continues to grow."

"You were still feeling it when we found you?"

"I was. It was getting worse by the second." I glance quickly at Haarlem and then away again. "Screaming helped keep me sane, but it didn't do a thing for the terror."

Wes stands up decisively. "I'll cancel the overflights," he says, but he gives me a bitter look, and I know he is resentful because I have denied him this pleasure: flying over a land where no man has walked, seeing what no man has seen, knowing that no man will ever see it this way in the future, for virginity cannot be restored.

"I think the other party at the shore should be recalled," I say, but now I have gone too far. He shakes his head and presently leaves me with Haarlem.

"You did a crazy thing for someone not crazy," Haarlem says, but he is undressing as he speaks, and contentedly I move over and watch him.

The sun is out, and the perfection of this planet, this day, is such that I feel I could expand to the sky, fill the spaces between the ground and the heavens with my being, and my being is joyful. The air is pristine. The desire to pull off our impermeable suits is voiced by nearly everyone. To run naked in the fields, to love and be loved under the golden sun, to gather flowers and strew them about for our beds, to follow the meandering stream to the river and plunge into the cool, invisible water, where the rocks and plants on the bottom are as sharp and clear as those on the bank, these are our thoughts on this most glorious day.

An urgent message from the shore party shatters our euphoria. Tony has gone mad and has broken Francine's neck in his frenzy. He eluded the others and ran into the woods, leaving a trail of instruments behind him.

Wes has ordered the shore party to return to the ship. He has ordered me to the infirmary to wait for Francine, who is dying.

No one suggested we bury Francine. We have her body ready for space burial, and now we orbit the planet and monitor our instruments from a distance. The spy satellites will be finished in three days, and then we shall leave. We voted unanimously that the planet is uninhabitable, and that too will be a note in the paragraph in the catalogue of worlds. No one will come here again. There is no need for further exploration; no future seedling colonists will christen this world. The planet will forever remain a number.

Wes and I are awake, taking the first watch. Although we trust our instruments, our machines completely, we choose to have two humans awake at all times. Always before when I stood watch, it was with Haarlem, but this time I volunteered when Wes said he would be first. Haarlem didn't even look at me when I made the choice.

The Deep Sleep will erase the immediacy of the planet, melt it into the body of other planets, so that only by concentration will any of us be able to feel our experience here again. And there is something I must decide before I permit this to happen. Haarlem said, mockingly, "No one believes in heaven, or the Garden, but there is a system of responses to archetypes built into each of us, and this planet has triggered those responses."

I refuse to believe him. Our instruments failed to detect a presence, a menace, a being that made what appeared to be perfection in fact a death trap. I think of the other worlds to which we have condemned our colonists, worlds too hot, or too cold, with hostile animal life, or turbulent weather, and mutely I cry out that this planet that will remain forever a number in the catalogue of worlds is worse than any of them. None of the other worlds claimed a life, and this planet has taken four. But my dreams are troubled, and I think of the joy and serenity that we all felt, only to be overcome again by terror.

We all shared the fear. The thought races through my mind over and over. We all shared the fear. The best of us and the worst. Even I.

Even I.

Mrs. Bagley Goes to Mars

ON A DREARY Tuesday in March, Mrs. Bagley told her family she was going to Mars. It was a day exactly like all others—she always got up first, shook her husband, put on her robe, went to the kitchen to make coffee, pounded on Joey's door until he grunted, and then went to shower and dress, passing her husband who by then was finished with the bathroom. While she dressed and did her hair, Mr. Bagley and Joey had breakfast: cold cereal, juice she had made the night before, toast.

When she returned to the kitchen the air was smoky; a piece of burned toast lay soaking up spilled milk on the counter.

"Better take that toaster to the shop," her husband said, not looking up.

"Mom," Joey said, "you got that ten dollars?"

"What ten dollars?"

Mr. Bagley didn't look up.

"I told you. After school we get measured for caps and gowns. I gotta put ten down . . ."

Somewhere water was falling. A silver trickle kissed mossy rocks, a thundering cascade ripped house-sized boulders loose from the cliffs, crashed them down. . . .

". . . by six, I hope. Oh, yeah, can you spare a couple of bucks for gas?"

That was when she said, "I'm going to Mars."

Mr. Bagley, like a well-bred visitor who didn't overhear family matters, didn't look up.

Somewhere a star was going nova, a black hole was vacuuming space, a comet was combing its hair.

Mr. Bagley finished his cereal and pushed his bowl back. He had been talking. ". . . seven calls, at least. You won't be late if we leave now. Come on. You can eat at the cafeteria, can't you?"

"I haven't even had coffee yet!"

"You can drink it on the way to the bus. Come on or we'll both be late."

Her supervisor, Bentsen, said, "Mrs. Bagley, this is the third time in two weeks. Why?"

"It's rained three times these two weeks."

"We don't want to have to let you go, Mrs. Bagley, but . . ."

Somewhere a giraffe stretched out a purple tongue toward bright green leaves at the top of a tree. Somewhere a wound-down kitten slept on a pillow, like a fuzzy pom-pom.

At her machine she pressed a knee lever and green plastic flowed toward her. They were making tank covers, or bus covers; she was not certain just what they were making. Across from her Dolores was talking.

"Ellie and me, we're walking to catch our bus and it's warm in the terminal, you know. We're carrying our coats. And here comes this black dude, big, not really black, but like coffee that's half milk, and he's staring at Ellie's. You know? Me, I'm invisible when I'm with Ellie, like a star when the sun comes up, still there, but invisible. We're talking about killing Bentsen, that's all we ever talk about any more. And this dude is staring and grinning and making sucking faces. Ellie slows down and starts to stare too, right at his dingus, and he likes that fine, you can tell. Then Ellie starts to laugh and she laughs like she's going to bust something. And she tries to keep her eyes on him, but she can't, she's laughing too hard, and she puts her arm around me and puts her head on my shoulder, like one of *them*. You know? And that cat, he just vanishes, melts right into the floor. Never fails! That Ellie!"

Somewhere a father was holding up a little girl so she could glimpse a shiny train sliding silently through the silver night. Somewhere a spotted dog quivered as it listened to a school bus long before it came into sight.

"You don't feel so hot or something?" Dolores was leaning forward, looking at her.

"I'm okay. I'm going to Mars, you know."

"Like that place over in Jersey? I heard they keep you a week and do exams no one else even heard of yet. Same exams they give the astronauts, I heard. You'll be okay. It's not to worry." She glanced up and pressed her knee lever hard, causing a tidal wave of plastic to flow. Bentsen passed and Dolores said, "Tell you about this guy I met last night? Ellie and me was in this place . . ."

Somewhere a pink bird picked out the pink stones on a beach and laid a wall. Somewhere red sands sifted moonlight and starlight and rose hues bathed the land.

It rained on Wednesday, too.

"Mrs. Bagley, is there a problem?" The personnel supervisor was very young and pretty. She wore her hair down her back and when she put on her glasses to glance at the file before her, she looked like a child playing grown-up.

"I have sick leave coming, don't I?" Mrs. Bagley asked.

The girl ran her finger down the paper before her. She had silver polish on her long nails. "You haven't had time off for six years!"

"There are examinations, like they give the astronauts, I understand, and they keep you at least a week. A place over in Jersey."

"Oh dear! I do hope it isn't serious. There's a form here

somewhere you should have them fill out for us. Just routine."
She rummaged in her desk, got up and opened a file drawer and
extracted a paper. "Here we are. Now, let's just go over this
together, shall we? You have to fill out this part, see? Your name,
address, where you live at present . . ."

Somewhere rising smoke became a column that supported a
gray sky over a gray land. Somewhere a golden fish floated
among lily pads carelessly splashed with violet flowers.

"Mom, I told you! We have to pay today! It's for our graduation party, over at the shore!"

Joey held out his hand and Mrs. Bagley walked around it,
carrying dishes to the sink.

"I got seven calls today," Mr. Bagley said, dipping his doughnut into his coffee. "I can't make them all by bus."

Mrs. Bagley went to the bedroom to get her purse. Joey
followed, his hand still out, jiggling the car keys with his other
hand. She caught the keys and dropped them into her pocket.
"Ask your father," she said.

"He ain't got no money."

"I get paid today. I have to go to the bank after work."

"Hey! How'm I supposed to get to school?"

"Walk."

Mr. Bagley read the paper and dunked his doughnut. Joey
turned toward him, shrugged, and left the house, slamming the
door. "I ain't going to school today!"

"Why'd you take his keys?"

"They aren't his. They are mine. I'm paying for the car, insurance, everything, and I'm the one who rides the bus. Not
today."

"What are you mad about anyway? Because I got all them
calls to make? That make you mad?"

Mrs. Bagley returned to the bedroom and took off her coat;
she began to throw things out of her drawer onto the bed. She
would need all her underwear, all her knee hose, no curlers.

They didn't curl their hair on Mars.

"What in hell are you doing?"

"I'm going to Mars," Mrs. Bagley said. "I told you."

"You're crazy. Put that stuff away. You'll be late."

"Goodbye," Mrs. Bagley said. "I don't know how long I'll be away."

"You hear me? Put that stuff away."

Mrs. Bagley sat on the edge of the bed and presently Mr. Bagley said, "I've got to go. You sick or something? Call in sick. You got the time coming to you."

She didn't answer and after a moment he left for work. Mrs. Bagley finished packing, turned off the lights and the stove and left also.

At the plant she parked in the visitor section when she picked up her check. She went to the bank and withdrew a hundred dollars and cashed her check. Altogether she now had a little over two hundred dollars, enough, she hoped, to permit her to buy a little souvenir or two. In order not to be a burden on the flight people, she went to a supermarket and bought a few provisions for the trip—canned apple juice, some instant coffee, cheese, crackers and several candy bars. Satisfied, she drove toward Lincoln Tunnel and New Jersey.

It was almost dark when she pulled off the interstate and ate her crackers and cheese. She should have asked directions, she realized, but she had been so certain that she knew the way. As if she had glimpsed a map, or had gone before, she recognized the route as she reached various turns, but it would be comforting to have a map. She drank the apple juice, and with the food and drink, her certainty returned and she started to drive again.

Somewhere a ship was standing in moonlight, waiting. Somewhere the flight attendants were glancing at their watches, hoping she would not delay them too much.

She turned at Kittatinny Mountain and there on the side of the road was her guide, waving to her. When he opened the car door, the overhead light came on and he hesitated, glanced in the back seat, then back down the road she had just driven.

"It's all right," she said. "I've been expecting you." Not really *him,* she told herself, someone. "You do know the way, don't you?"

He got in, but kept very close to the door, pressing against it with his back in such a way that he could look at her, out the back window, back to her. "Way to where?"

"To the ship."

She hoped he wouldn't sense her disappointment in his appearance. But of course, they would look like everyone else, or their lives would be endangered.

"I've always known I'd get to go," Mrs. Bagley said. "I used to read about space and Mars, all that, when I was a girl, and once I stood out on the sidewalk and crossed my arms and tried wishing myself up, but nothing happened." The road was narrow and unmarked and she was driving slowly, braking for curves, pulling over as far as she could whenever a car approached. There was little traffic. Woods grew close to the road on both sides here, and the farm house lights were far apart. The road started to climb and she slowed more.

"You turn right up there," the guide said. He had stopped looking out the rear window, was watching her. This road was even narrower and no light at all showed.

"I suppose you were excited when you found that you were coming to Earth," Mrs. Bagley said. "It is a surprise, in a way, but not really. It's like finding something you lost a long time ago, but always felt would turn up again."

"You turn again soon," he said. "Left." He leaned forward, watching the road. "Now."

This was hardly more than a trail. Mrs. Bagley concentrated on driving. There were water-filled holes that reflected her headlights and she couldn't guess how deep they were.

"Stop," her guide said, and his voice seemed changed, deeper and thicker.

Mrs. Bagley stopped and turned off the engine, switched off the lights. She could see nothing beyond the car, could only see the outline of the man against the darkness outside, could see something gleam briefly.

"Now don't you start yelling or nothing . . ."

But she wasn't listening to him. "Look!" she cried. "Look at it! It's beautiful. Come on! They're waiting." She pushed the door open and jumped out, ran toward the ship.

On Mars they allowed her to rest several minutes before they began tests to see what occupation would be suitable for her. She soon found herself installed before a machine that heat-seamed plastic to make covers for tanks, or buses, or something. The plastic was red; she operated the machine with her elbow, and the operator across from her was not Dolores.

She listened to the tongue-twisting monologue of not/Dolores until the coffee break, and then she told her supervisor she was returning to Earth.

They were sorry to lose her, they said sibilantly, but they understood. It must be very difficult to be the only Earthman on Mars. They never did understand she was a female: all Earth persons looked alike to them. "You are born," they said. "You ingest food, defecate, mature, reproduce, grow old and die. All of you alike."

Mrs. Bagley shook her head. "Your sources are wrong," she said. "Women, females, ladies, one half the population or even a little bit more don't defecate. You won't find that in your sources. They go to the little girls' room, or the powder room, or ladies' room. They freshen up, or wash their hands, or fix their make-up, but they never shit."

The Martians, hissing with bewilderment over this incomprehensible difference between the male and female organisms of the Earth species, returned to their sources. They saw Mrs. Bagley off regretfully, she thought, but did not attempt to detain her. They even returned the price of her ticket since she had not stayed the seventy-two-hour trial period.

The ship landed on the spot where she had embarked, and she stood for a short time looking at the discarded body of her former guide. It was clever of them to assume a human form and then abandon it this way, making it look like a dreadful accident, or even a homicide. No one would bother to probe deeply into the death of a bum found with a knife in his heart.

She backed out the lane carefully, made her turn and retraced her drive back home. Mr. Bagley was reading the Sunday papers when she entered the apartment.

"How's your sister?" he asked, not looking up.

"I haven't seen her."

"You ain't kidding me. You think I don't know where you been? Where else would you go?" He folded the paper and started on the comics.

"Did you call her?"

"And give you that satisfaction? You kidding?"

"Where's Joey?"

"Out somewhere."

Mrs. Bagley unpacked her suitcase and put away her things, then she started dinner.

On Monday a light drizzle was falling.

"Look, Mom, it ain't fair! I gotta pick up Suzanne and Eddie and take them to the jewelry store for their rings, and we gotta . . ."

Somewhere a dragon, breathing heavily, seared a shishkabob for its beloved. Somewhere a butterfly squirmed from its sleeping bag and stretched first one then the other emerald wing, and yawned.

"When you go to the store, get me some shaving cream, will you? And we're out of toothpaste, and my tan suit needs to go to the cleaners. And get that damn toaster fixed." Mr. Bagley spoke with his mouth full and didn't look at her, but marked his place in the newspaper with one finger, then resumed reading. Joey left, slamming the door.

"You got some change? I'm going to be in the Bronx all day, can't get to the bank."

She handed him a ten-dollar bill and he grunted and turned the page to the sports section.

"You better have a talk with Joey when he gets home. Out all night Saturday. To be expected when his old lady stays out all weekend. I don't like it, though, telling you." He scanned the scores, talking, eating, dripping coffee.

Somewhere rainbow-colored clouds swirled gently, thick enough to float on, to ride to earth. Somewhere a new flower opened and stared at the sun wide-eyed.

". . . the hell you do, but you could let us know. . . ."

She went to the living room and started to gather dirty clothes, Joey's sweater and socks, an ashtray filled with candy wrappers, beer cans. . . .

When she heard the door close, she dropped the dirty clothes and sat on the couch. She picked up the classified section of the paper and, at first idly, then with more attention, began to read the Help Wanted column.

It was still drizzling when Mrs. Bagley left the apartment and took the bus to the station where she could catch a train to Long Island. Ganymede, she thought, that was the answer. Mars had been too close, too like Earth, but Ganymede was different.

On Ganymede they showed her an efficiency that was to be hers, and a native explained her duties to her, wished her luck and left her alone. Here they lived in immense apartments, with plush carpeting and futuristic furniture, and they spoke another language so they could not jabber at her. She was to clean the apartments for them.

She sat down and turned on her own nine-inch television set and leaned back. Somewhere, she thought, dirty clothes were rising to the ceiling, and smoke was curling up from the bottom of the heap. Somewhere dishes were growing strange molds—gray, green, blue. Somewhere a man in an undershirt was jamming a coffee-soaked doughnut into his ear.

Later, when the building was silent and dark, she went to the street and checked one more time, and it was still there: Ganymede Arms. She went back to her room and to bed knowing they would never find her on Ganymede.

Symbiosis

BEACHAM, INDIANA, has 1,200 people, a train station that has no passenger service, a main street called Davenport Street, with a Woolworth's, a hamburger joint, Penney's, Wesson's hardware, Stuart's department store, a Jack and Jill shop, and a bakery. There is an ice-cream bar in the drugstore, and a gas station, and then you're out of downtown. The post office is a block south, and across the street from it is the municipal park with its cannon and a few benches pigeon-spattered and three oak trees. They are the only trees downtown. Town Hall is through the park, across First Street. The building is flush with the sidewalk, not set back at all. A red brick building with gray, wide stairs, and heavy double doors with brass hinges. The school is out of town, a cooperative school that serves the whole county. Every morning the yellow bus makes the run through town, then vanishes with the town's children, a mechanized Pied Piper, expelling exhaust fumes as it strips gears and groans and races its engine.

As soon as the children are old enough, or look old enough, they pile up in cars and race up through the county to Valparaiso, where they spend their movie and soda money on beer or the drive-in, and the girls pick up boys and the boys leer at the local girls. They all know that our town is deadly, that it is out to get them. When they really are old enough, after the graduation exercises and the dance that goes on all night, with the morning light revealing drunk kids in cars, or on porch swings, or on each other's couches or, if the party was exceptionally "good," in jail, then they go off to college, or the Army, and they vanish for good. Most of them never come back.

Through town, down Third Street, past the doctor's office, my father's office, on through four more blocks and out of town for a mile and a half to the McInally farm. Laura McInally and I have been friends for all our lives. We went to school together, the same Baptist church that is near her farm—our town is almost universally Protestant, except for the fourteen Jewish families who go to Rensselaer to the synagogue, and the hundred or so Italian families who go to the Catholic church. Laura and I used to walk past the tiny Catholic church and pretend that we were being captured and carried inside, forced to don nuns' clothes, mistreated by the nun in charge, and threatened constantly by the priests who used young Protestant girls most shamefully. We would pull our hair back tight and try to imagine what we would look like with it all shaved off. We were certain that they would do that to us. What else they would do we never actually put into words, but rather talked all around it with ellipses.

David McInally, Laura's father, was a kind, red-faced man, who seemed to keep stores of tidbits in various pockets. His winter coat had nuts and caramels. His blue denim jacket had chewing gum. His tan work pants would yield lollipops. He was always surprised to find them there, and would hand them out as if glad to get rid of them. His life was regulated by corn. He had seven hundred acres planted in corn. He raised a few head of beef cattle, chickens, ducks, hogs; and he built: barns, silos, sheds, garages, a machine shop to care for his constantly growing fleet of farm machinery. The house was seventy years old and the kitchen had been remodeled once in the late forties.

Other than that and the repairs that kept it from falling down, and occasional paint it never got touched.

It wasn't a secret that Laura was his favorite of the four children. He wouldn't let her carry in kindling wood, or take out garbage, or walk to the bus stop half a mile away. There never had been a thing that she said she wanted that he didn't get for her, almost instantly. Let the boys do it, was constantly on his lips. There was girl work and there was boy work, and he wouldn't have her doing any boy work, even after the boys had left home and she was as strong as a teen-aged boy anyway, and willing to do the small chores that her brothers had always done. But he wouldn't let her. Also he wouldn't let her stay out after dark, or sleep over at my house, or play rough games, or ride a bicycle to school, or take an overnight trip to Chicago with our class. It was a two-sided blade.

Mrs. McInally was pretty. As far back as I can remember I thought she was pretty. She had pale brown hair that curled around her face, and her eyes were bright blue. Her hands and feet were very small. Laura and I went through a period of awkwardness when we realized that our feet were larger than her mother's. She was plump, as a baby is. Her wrists were tiny, then her arms grew rounder until at the elbow they were dimpled and boneless-looking. Her fat legs tapered to shapely ankles and her waist was as small as mine, an hourglass figure that looked very pretty all the time. She sewed beautifully and made all of her own clothes; her dresses were gay and bright, even her Sunday best. She was like a fat little partridge with a mono-bosom, drawn-in waistline, round hips. I remember her as eternally busy, and all her business was centered on her family and home. There never was any question about where she was, everyone knew. She hummed in a monotone, and sometimes told very innocent, naïve jokes. She mothered everyone. Since my own mother had died when I was six, she mothered me, lavishing kisses and good will and hospitality and love indiscriminately on her own children and me. Whenever she picked up a piece of material for a dress for Laura, she got one for me, too. Blue checks, white daisies on a field of blue, red candy stripes. I can remember every dress she ever made for me. All lovingly made up, beautifully finished and decorated with her own touches. An appliqué, or a bit of lace, or a ruffle. I gave her nothing in return. It never occurred to me that I should. I accepted her love just as her own children did.

All the McInally children had inherited their father's features: they were blue-eyed, with long noses and full lips. But the curious thing was the way their eyes were set in the face. They hardly were sunken at all, as if the eye sockets were too shallow to accommodate them, so the whole eye was forced out even with the cheeks. Laura wore sunglasses almost constantly from the time she was fourteen. She could never be pretty, or even very attractive, with them off, but with them on, she was lovely. Her figure was probably the best in our class, her legs long and smooth and beautiful. I used to exercise, trying to get that same look, and never came near it. Her hair was sun-bleached to a near platinum blond. Every winter it darkened, and we both mourned for it, then the spring sunshine worked its magic and the darkness disappeared.

We graduated together and signed up for Purdue in September. All that summer we sewed and made handbags, and shopped for boots and new coats and gloves in Indianapolis. Mrs. McInally worked as hard as we did to get us ready for college. Poor Mr. McInally couldn't stand the "damn female flitterings from morning to night." He spent his summer with his hands in the fields, or in the barns.

Later I could reconstruct the changes that had been taking place in Mrs. McInally over the past few years, but they were too gradual at the time for comment. There were two older brothers, and a sister, all of them gone now. The first brother worked for a plastics firm in New York. The next one was in the Navy, making it his career. The sister lived in Los Angeles with her husband. As each one left, Mrs. McInally had become busier than ever with the ones remaining. By the time Laura was the only one at home, Mrs. McInally was feverishly busy on her account.

In August my father told me that he was giving up his practice in Beacham, that he was going to study in Chicago and specialize in ocular allergies. Also, he was going to be married. I really looked at him for the first time in years, I suppose. He was forty-eight then, overworked as a small town doctor is, but a handsome-enough man, stooped, almost bald, slack muscles now from inactivity, but potentially very nice. I cried and he had a tear or two and we talked all night and had breakfast, and that afternoon I met his fiancée, who was his age and a doctor. I was shocked and relieved that she was so old. They had met at a symposium in Chicago. They planned to marry as soon as I got settled down in school. I cried a little bit more, and we all ended up kissing each other.

The McInallys invited me to spend weekends and holidays with them that year. I said I wasn't sure yet, and we let it go at that. I realized that Beacham was no longer my home, never would be again, and with the thought I began to look at it with new eyes. The town was ugly, I learned that summer. I hadn't really known it before. It was ugly and dull, and the land around it was dull. Flat cornland as far as one could see. During most of the year there was nothing there but gray fields, or snow fields, then the burst of green that gradually faded to brown and disappeared. The wind was louder than I had realized before. In August the corn was six to eight feet high, and when the wind blew in from the west, it was like the blizzard wind, the same high-pitched wail, the same rustling, of corn, not snow. The stores were ugly, neglected. The hot west and south summer winds and the sun that turned the sky white were merciless, fading, bleaching, blistering paint. In the winter the white of the sky reflected the land, and the winds were brutal. Nothing stayed pointed or smooth. Everything developed a sameness. The park was hideous with its bare ground and its scraggly bushes that no one ever pruned or fertilized or sprayed. The leaves were riddled: some were black with fungus or black spot disease. The benches were grimy, never used.

Laura and I walked through town repeatedly, as if to imprint its ugliness on our brains so that we never would be tempted to return. I was going to study biology, and she was majoring in mathematics. She had a natural aptitude for mathematics that had been noticeable from the time she entered elementary school. None of the processes was ever a mystery to her; she knew intuitively how to add, subtract, how to derive a formula, how to do trig problems. In high school I'd do her essays and she'd do my algebra. It seemed fair enough then.

School frightened both of us more than anything else we had known. We knew each other and a sprinkling of other kids who had come from our county, and no one else. In our town we had known everybody. And from being high among the top third of the class effortlessly, we suddenly had to work. Everyone in college had been top third. My first test paper with a D on it shook me. And Laura sat up three nights in a row studying for a French test, getting tighter and tighter on bennies. She made a C. We both pulled in and settled down to do some serious work, and it was Christmas.

On Christmas Day I was embarrassed by the largess of the McInallys. I had bought them a silver candy dish, and they gave me presents that only a daughter could expect. I didn't know how to accept such presents, and knew that I had to, but they were paying very little attention to me then. Both parents' eyes were riveted with embarrassing intensity on Laura as she unwrapped gift after gift; my glance at them was an invasion of privacy. I watched Laura, too, then. There was a bewildering array of jewelry, sweaters, curler sets, bags, belts, records, and on and on and on. And finally there was a fur coat.

"Mother! Dad! Are you both crazy!" Laura jumped up and put it on, twisting, dancing in it, burying her hands and her face in the soft pelt. It was a tawny-colored mink, the most beautiful coat I had ever seen. It was almost exactly the color of her hair in the middle of the winter. "You can't do something like this!" she cried, but to take it from her then would have been barbaric. Mrs. McInally had tears in her eyes, and Mr. McInally began to search frantically for a match for his cigar. I had matches in my pocket and I started to approach him with a package, but he found his and then put the cigar down. Mrs. McInally and Laura were examining the coat by then, and I found myself studying Laura's father. The expression on his face was strange, as if he were holding his breath. But of course he wasn't doing anything of the sort. He watched his wife with an anxious look, and I realized with a feeling of sickness that he was afraid. My stomach felt queasy suddenly as I watched him watch his wife. All the cheer that he had been showing was gone and his ugly eyes looked fierce, and afraid, the way he had looked afraid one time when the bull got loose and Laura was in the same pasture on her pony, the same quietness that was all tension ready to spring. Then it was over and Laura was insisting that I try on the coat and the incident seemed so out of step with everything else happening that I was willing to believe that I had imagined it all.

Laura and I were busy all through the holidays, all our friends were in town, and there were parties and skating parties and sledding, and dances in each other's basements. It was as if we were desperately picking up our past again, knowing we couldn't do it many more times. Then back to Purdue for our midyear finals.

"Laura," I said the first night back in our dormitory, "your mother looked tired, didn't she?"

"She's always pooped by Christmas. She must have baked a ton of fruitcakes and cookies. She puts in weeks on decorating the house. You know."

"I guess." And God help me, I forgot the whole thing.

Neither of us covered ourselves with glory that first semester, but neither were we put on probation, so we decided that we were holding our own. Summer came closer and I had to decide what to do with myself. I couldn't accept being a houseguest for the whole summer vacation; finally I enrolled for courses and when school was out, Laura went home and I stayed on at Purdue, after a short holiday with my father and his new wife. We were all very polite; that was the lasting impression that I took from the week with them. In August I went to the McInally farm for two weeks.

Everything was exactly as it had been from my first recollection of the place. Even to Morris, the hired hand, who never said anything, but grinned happily at us all. On a fairly regular basis Laura was dating Stephen Rodman, home from Harvard. Not exactly going steady, but almost.

One night, two days before we were to leave for school again, I woke up with my heart pounding hard, and prickles on my arms and legs. My mouth was dry and for a long time I couldn't move, then I managed to lift my head and I saw Mrs. McInally. She was sitting in a chair near the window, watching Laura.

She got up immediately and moved toward the door. "I just came in to check," she whispered, but she lied. She had been sitting there. How long? I stared at the ceiling, unable until dawn to return to sleep.

At breakfast she said to Laura, "Billy Washburn called again last night."

"Pretty Billy?" Laura giggled and spread apple jelly on toast.

"Don't call him that. He's a very nice boy."

"Oh, Mother!"

"Well, from what I hear about the Rodman boy and from what I know about Billy, I'd say that you could do worse. You could."

"Mother!" Laura refused to comment further. But the inflection, her disdain, the way she dismissed the idea without another word, it was clear that Pretty Billy was not her idea of date material.

Billy Washburn had graduated with us, by the grace of most

of his teachers. He always had been the best-looking boy in school, large, well-built, excellent in all sports, voted most popular boy. He worked for his father, who had a first-rate mechanic shop. Billy wanted no more than that. He never dreamed of leaving Beacham. I thought of him and Laura and smiled. With her sunglasses and her mink coat and boots she looked just like a starlet.

I didn't go back to the McInally farm for over a year. I went to Jamaica with my father and his wife for Christmas, and at midterm I stayed with them in Chicago. We weren't all being so very polite to each other anymore and they both had wanted me, that was clear. Laura didn't want to go home. Her mother was driving her crazy, she said. Menopause, you know. She stared broodingly at the wall, then shrugged. She went down to Fort Lauderdale for Easter with friends from school, so I went back to Chicago, without even thinking about asking this time. I simply called and said when I'd be there and that was that. Later I had to smile at my first impression of his wife; she was really very nice and quite attractive, and not at all old. We were becoming very good friends. That summer I stayed with them and took some courses at Northwestern.

In our third year Laura began to show signs of restiveness. She talked about changing her major, about dropping out entirely, about joining the Peace Corps for a year or two. She was doing beautiful work, and was on full scholarship now, with her future so assured that to talk about changing anything was insane. Suddenly corners were being cut for her, red tape was fading away, the drudgery of undergraduate work was being shelved. I was frankly envious, but she was cynical about it.

"They want to use me," she said. "I'm a thing to them. A thing they can hone up and use. I just don't want it. What if I can't do what they want? Then what? The junk pile?"

"What are you talking about? You've never failed yet and you know it."

"Yeah, that was different. I've got a headache. You don't

know how they're pressuring me now. You just don't know. I'd just like to get away from everything, everyone."

We had a blizzard a week before Thanksgiving that year, catching everyone unprepared; the department of roads didn't have the plows out yet, the school didn't have its snow shovels out. Instant chaos. The school closed early for the Thanksgiving holiday.

"Come home with me," Laura said, sitting on her bed, packed, ready to leave. Billy Washburn was coming for her.

"Can't. I told Dad I'd be in Chicago."

"That's silly. You'd have to sit in this dump for the next three or four days until they get everything unsnarled. Come on. Call him up and tell him. He'll say it's the smartest thing to do."

Actually it was. We had a ride. Billy said the roads to Beacham were all right, but it didn't really matter, we all had driven in snow up to the windows of the car practically.

When I still hesitated, Laura said, "Please do. I'm worried about Mother. I keep thinking it's my imagination, but then I see her, and I know it isn't."

"What's wrong?"

"That's just it. I don't know. Come see if you think there's anything."

So I packed to go to the country instead of to the city. When Billy got there it was snowing again. Laura sat beside Billy in the front seat and I had the back seat to myself. Her hair and the mink coat blended until it was hard to tell where one left off and the other began. She baited him all the way home. Billy didn't respond to her thrusts at all. He simply drove with concentration, and a scene from the past spring came to mind. It had been one of those times when a crusading editor, or reporter, or trustee decides to stir up a hornet's nest by announcing that the women's dorm is a den of iniquity. There had been investigations and visits by the local firemen of the administration and all that. And in our room one night, lights out, Laura and I had talked about it, laughing, but with undercurrents of self-mockery. We were both still virgins, although we would have died before telling any of the investigators that.

"If I do decide to go all the way," Laura said, "it'll be with Pretty Billy."

"For heaven's sake! Why that creep?"

"Because I can wind him around my finger. He'd do exactly what I told him to do. Like the knight whose lady told him he had to quit defending her, all that crap. He had to obey and he couldn't, so there was no way out except suicide."

"Good God, Laura, pick on someone your own size!"

"I mean it," she said. "If you let someone that you care about too much, it'll lead to nothing but trouble. I ought to know." Stephen Rodman had become engaged to a Bryn Mawr girl suddenly, after almost going steady with Laura for a couple of years.

I watched her head, and the back of Billy's head, and I knew she had done it. Neither of us had brought it up again when we got back to the dorm in September. When we got very near the sort of conversation that would have led to confessions, we both had scrambled to change the subject simultaneously. I hadn't been willing to let her know that she had been right. I had cared, and it had led to trouble. She obviously had not cared.

Beacham had become stranger and stranger to me, and seeing it that day, springing up out of the blinding snow, was like glimpsing an alien landscape. No humans would have huddled their hideous buildings together like that with so much open country around them. They couldn't have chosen to crowd into such a small area. There must have been monsters out there for them to guard against. The monster was the silence and the emptiness, I thought as we went through town and out again, back into the empty farm country.

Then we were at the farm and Mr. and Mrs. McInally were bustling about helping us off with boots, coats, putting hot toddies into our hands, everyone talking, laughing, and it felt like a homecoming. Morris stood against the wall grinning, saying

nothing. Later I studied Mrs. McInally and I knew that there
was something wrong. She had lost a lot of weight, but it was
more than that. Two days later I realized that she no longer was
pretty and tidy and gay. Her clothes were subtly wrong, not
starched, or not ironed fastidiously, or not matched with her
aprons just so. Little things here and there. Hard in themselves
to find and label wrong, but with a cumulative effect of strange-
ness. And Mr. McInally was nervous. I wondered if he was what
was wrong with his wife. He fidgeted with his pipe, he couldn't
sit still, he started at a loud noise, and twice he got up to go to
the barn because he was afraid the roof had blown down, or that
a cow was bawling, or something.

Then one night when Laura was out with Billy, Mrs. McInally
sat down by me and took out her crocheting and said, "I guess
she'll marry him, won't she?"

"Billy?"

"Yes. Has she said anything about it to you?"

"No. Not a word."

"That's funny. She always was like that, closemouthed when
it came to her own plans."

I stared at the page before me, but I wasn't reading. And later
when Laura and I were in our room and everyone else was
sleeping, I asked her.

"Marry Pretty Billy! You're off your nut!"

"That's what I thought. But your mother seems to think you
will."

"Damn it. She probably knows to the minute when I lost my
wonderful state of innocence." We both heard footsteps in the
hall then and became quiet. I heard those steps during the night
all the time that I was there.

On Sunday night, before we left, Mrs. McInally said to me,
"It's such a shame that your father left us. We all miss him so
much."

"Are you sick?" I asked before I thought.

"No!" She said it so quickly that it became a self-contradic-
tion. Mr. McInally took a step to her side unconsciously, his

•

hand out, reaching for her arm. Laura came in then and there was nothing else. We all kissed each other and Laura and I left with Billy.

"She is sick," I said to Laura late that night.

"She says she isn't. She says it's the change, that the doctor is giving her something. And Dad says she's fine."

Three weeks later Mrs. McInally tried to kill herself and her husband.

I came back to the dorm at ten. Laura was hysterical, trying to get some clothes into her suitcase. "Mother's sick. They took her to the hospital. I have to go. Goddamn it, where's my other shoe?"

"Laura, sit down. Let me do it. What happened?"

So we both began to throw things into the suitcase, because she couldn't sit down. Finally I got out the emergency bottle and gave her a drink of bourbon and Coke and she lighted a cigarette and let me finish.

"Do you have a ride arranged?"

"Billy. He's on his way. He'll take me. . . ."

"I'll come too, Laura. You might need me. Your father might need someone there while you two are at the hospital. How serious is it? Was it a heart attack? What happened?"

She shook her head. "I don't know. You can't come, not now. She's in . . . she's in intensive care. We can't even see her yet. Dad told me. I'll be with him." She put out her cigarette and began rummaging in her purse for another one. She wouldn't look at me.

"Laura, there must be something I can do. I'll make coffee and keep it hot. Something."

"No! You can't come! Mind your own business!" Then she burst into tears. "Don't you understand anything? She's in Hillside Hospital."

Then I understood. Hillside Hospital was in Indianapolis. It was for mental patients. I must have stood shaking my head for a long time.

"She had a breakdown," Laura said, after a while. "She

turned on the stove and tried to kill them both." She laughed
shrilly. "In that old house she would have had to leave it on for
a month for enough gas to accumulate to do any harm."

She didn't have her sunglasses on. Her face was red from
crying, her eyes bulging and red-rimmed. I gave her another
drink, and had one myself. "When Dad woke up, she tried to
hit him with whatever she could pick up. She was throwing
everything not nailed down. I think he's cut up a little. He said
something about stitches. He yelled for Morris to call the doctor
and he got her and held her on the floor until the doctor got
there and gave her a shot." She looked at me with a hopeless
expression. "We knew, didn't we? Dad knew. He lied to me
about her. This has been coming on for a long time. And we all
knew something was wrong. And no one did anything at all."

There wasn't anything I could say. She left with Billy and I
didn't hear from her again until after the Christmas vacation.
I started to go to the hospital a dozen times, but I didn't. It
would have been an intrusion, I knew. I tried to call the farm
every day, thinking maybe they were home again, but no one
was. After I came back from Chicago, Laura turned up. She was
pale and thin and haunted-looking.

"They're giving her shock treatments," she said. She was
trembling. That was all she would say about it. She took her
finals and did brilliantly, as expected. Then she went home for
midterm, and again I was excluded. No one could see Mrs.
McInally, there was no point in my being there.

I didn't think Laura would come back for the second semester, but she did. Gray-faced, haggard, she studied fiercely, and
each weekend Billy came to fetch her home. Her mother was
being allowed visitors finally.

In March Laura said I could go with her to the hospital. I had
my car by then, so I drove, and she smoked continually all the
way, and said nothing.

The hospital was red brick, and the windows were barred, but
I had known that. There was an outer gate and a gatehouse that

had an attendant who stopped us and looked at our identification and then waved us through. Laura sat stiffly upright, staring ahead. The grounds were barren-looking, it was the season for barrenness. The sky was dirty gray and the air foul with smoke and haze and dirt. Although the heater worked perfectly, I was chilled. We drove around the main building, to Admissions, and went inside to get passes for the women's wing. We drove again on the winding roads with the remains of the winter's snows in black piles along the shoulders. Neither of us spoke, except when Laura told me to turn left, or right, or straight ahead to the parking lot. We walked back to the women's building and again had to stop, to show our passes this time, and to wait for the head nurse to verify our purpose. She was a large woman with soft gray hair and hard blue eyes. We signed her book and waited while she went back inside her office and used her telephone. Then we were allowed inside the corridor that led to the wing where Mrs. McInally was. What I had thought was a door was really a reinforced, locked gate that had to be opened and closed for each visitor. A second nurse accompanied us down the corridor past wards with neat beds in three rows, head to foot to head. Each bed had a brown cover folded at the foot, and each had a white nightstand at the head. It was very neat. A ring of keys jangled from the nurse's belt.

The floor was brown linoleum, brown and tan squares, hopscotch, or checkers, or chess. Two women were on their knees scrubbing the floor near a closed door. They wore gray dresses. One looked up at us and smiled, she had three upper teeth, none at all below. "It's better for them to stay busy," the nurse said, leading us. I glanced again at the women. They kept scrubbing the same spot. *What damned spot?* I thought, and pulled my coat tighter. The nurse stopped at a closed door. All the doors were metal, the walls tan, the floors brown, the doors gunmetal gray. The door was opened by another nurse who admitted us and closed the door after us. She turned a key in it. Then she announced, "McInally, company."

The room had a concrete floor, stone walls. Long tables made a U, open at the door side. Women were seated at the tables, some of them talking to company, some of them alone, doing nothing. A few were doing needlework, knitting, crocheting, embroidering. One was coloring a child's coloring book, with scraps of crayons. Another was painting. All of them wore shapeless faded dresses, not all the same, but of a kind. Cheap gingham, simply made to fit all from size ten to sixteen, or even eighteen. There were high windows that had no curtains. The windows were very clean. The whole place was tidy and clean, obsessively clean. As if all the energy of the place went into keeping it tidy and clean.

Mrs. McInally came from behind the table to our right. She looked hesitatingly at the nurse, seeking permission. The nurse nodded and she came forward, walking carefully, as if recovering from a back injury, and held out her hands to Laura. "How pretty you look," she said. "Where are your glasses? Wear your glasses, child, or your eyes will hurt you. You know that."

I don't know if she saw me or not. She didn't look at me at all. When I spoke to her she didn't answer.

"Come with me," she said, drawing Laura with her. "I'm making something for you. Come see." Again that strange, stiff walk, her head up a little too high, her neck too rigid.

We followed her around the table to her chair. "That's mine," she said, pointing to a small wicker basket on the table. She felt around in it without looking, now she was eyeing her neighbors suspiciously. "They steal my things in here," she said, not lowering her voice at all. "They know I have pretty things for you and they want them. Here they are." She held up dime-store beads that were partially strung. "I'm making it for you," she said again.

"Mother, they're very pretty. Are you feeling all right? Are you eating, sleeping?"

She shook her head and looked warningly at the nurse at the door. "I'm fine," she said brightly. "Just fine."

She had lost thirty pounds at least. Her little partridge bosom was nothing but skin now, and the plump hips were straight lines from her waist down. Her face was angular, and her eyes deep-sunken. She looked very ill. Her dress was buttoned wrong, leaving a gap in the middle of her chest, and an extra button at the top. And her hair was straggly and full of bobby pins in an effort to keep it back. But the bobby pins had been put in without a mirror and most of them were in the wrong places. She went from her aware, suspicious expression to a half-asleep one suddenly.

"I'll brush your hair, Mother," Laura said. She took a brush from her purse and began to remove the bobby pins. Her mother sat down, looking vacantly ahead. Another woman sidled close to Laura and felt her hair tentatively. Laura stiffened, but didn't pull away.

After our visit we sat in the car not speaking, smoking quietly for several minutes, then I started the motor. "She lived for over a year believing that her next step would put her in hell," Laura said softly. Her hand with the cigarette shook. "She could see it burning in front of her, sulphurous flames and smoke waiting to engulf her. She couldn't sleep because she was so afraid the house would catch on fire from it. She would get up at all hours to make sure nothing was burning. Sometimes she inhaled the smoke, then she would cough for hours. Every time she walked, she was braving hell itself. She didn't dare look at her feet. As long as she didn't look, she could make herself walk about, but if she looked, then she froze. Dad knew that. That she froze. Sometimes he'd find her unable to move, staring at the floor in front of her, and he'd pick her up and carry her to bed."

I drove slowly, meticulously, glad that I had it to do. Laura said, after lighting another cigarette, "He was afraid to doubt her when she said there was nothing wrong. He forced himself to believe her. She was going to Dr. Tom Dooley. He really believed that it would pass, that Dr. Dooley was taking care of her."

"Have you talked to the hospital doctor yet?"

"Nothing. They make no promises. At least she's quiet. Tranquilizers, of course. She was violent when they took her in. Poor Dad, he threw her down into hell and held her there until the doctor arrived. She may never forgive him."

All the gaiety and spontaneity died in Laura that spring. She studied determinedly and went to the hospital on the weekends. That was her life. I went back with her three more times, and then we both agreed that there was no point in my going again. Mrs. McInally simply refused to acknowledge me. I began to feel that it was deliberate on her part, that somehow I had been made the heavy, just as Mr. McInally had been. The doctors had asked him not to visit her until they told him it was all right. His visits were upsetting to her. The other children came now and then, but they were busy and distant, and their visits were necessarily limited.

They gave her mother another series of shock treatments late in the spring, and this time, according to Laura, it helped. We separated at the end of the semester reluctantly, as if we both knew that a whole phase of our lives had ended and the changes that were taking place would become more and more all-encompassing. When the new semester began in September, Laura wasn't there.

I had heard from her during the summer, brief, not very communicative cards. I worked for a biological testing firm in Maine, so I hadn't had a chance to visit the farm, or the hospital. I got a note from Laura finally in October; she was through with school.

I drove to the farm that weekend.

"It's no good," Laura said, at the car door. "Go on back. Just don't try to talk me into anything. I'm fed up with everyone trying to talk me into things."

"I didn't come for that. How is your mother? Is she home?"

"Yes. Come on in. Only you can't stay more than half an hour or so." She was wearing tight pants and a jersey, thin and hard as a model, as taut and strung out as a bowstring. She wasn't wearing her sunglasses. Her mother was not well. I don't know why they let her out, but I could see very little difference from how she had been the last time I had seen her at the hospital. My visit was very brief. Mr. McInally was cordial, obviously pleased to see me. Mrs. McInally glanced at me once, then ignored me. She still didn't look down, although her avoidance wasn't quite as noticeable as it had been. She was less stiff, but it was still there, and she knew it, and she had decided to live with it. Maybe that was easier than the hospital and shock treatment. I looked at Laura, who knew that I knew. She didn't move a muscle anywhere. True or not true, she wasn't going to acknowledge anything now.

She walked back to the car with me. I started to get in, then stopped and threw my arms around her. I was weeping, but she was cool and calm.

"You'd better get started," she said. "We'll get heavy fog tonight. It's that time of year. You don't want to have to drive in it."

She married Billy in the winter sometime. There was no wedding to speak of, from what I heard. They went to a Justice of the Peace, and then went back to the farm. She had a baby in April.

I am still in touch with other people from Beacham, and they tell me how it is with her and her mother. It's been five years now; she has five children. She must have learned that you can't count on four being enough. Her mother recovered, apparently, marvelous what the doctors at Hillside did for her, but poor Mr. McInally leads a dog's life. They both pick at him constantly. I imagine Mrs. McInally walking around with her head up, her eyes straight ahead, restless at night, sniffing. Billy isn't around much. There's talk about a girl. With Billy there will always be talk about a girl. Laura has gained a lot of weight, and never wears sunglasses anymore. I don't go back there. Mrs. McInally still thinks I'm one of them, the ones who tried to take her child from her. And Laura wouldn't want to see me now.

I know she wouldn't want to see me. I understand that she is very busy with church work. That and the children take all her time. She never even has time to go into town anymore. The last time she did, three or four years ago, she had such a bad asthma attack that they thought she might die. She couldn't stop coughing for days. They say she is a beautiful mother.

Ladies and Gentlemen, This Is Your Crisis

4 P.M. Friday

LOTTIE'S FACTORY closed early on Friday, as most of them did now. It was four when she got home, after stopping for frozen dinners, bread, sandwich meats, beer. She switched on the wall TV screen before she put her bag down. In the kitchen she turned on another set, a portable, and watched it as she put the food away. She had missed four hours.

They were in the mountains. That was good. Lottie liked it when they chose mountains. A stocky man was sliding down a slope, feet out before him, legs stiff—too conscious of the camera, though. Lottie couldn't tell if he had meant to slide, but he did not look happy. She turned her attention to the others.

A young woman was walking slowly, waist high in ferns, so apparently unconscious of the camera that it could only be a pose this early in the game. She looked vaguely familiar. Her blond hair was loose, like a girl in a shampoo commercial, Lottie decided. She narrowed her eyes, trying to remember where she had seen the girl. A model, probably, wanting to be a star. She would wander aimlessly, not even trying for the prize, content with the publicity she was getting.

The other woman was another sort altogether. A bit over-weight, her thighs bulged in the heavy trousers the contestants wore; her hair was dyed black and fastened with a rubber band in a no-nonsense manner. She was examining a tree intently. Lottie nodded at her. Everything about her spoke of purpose, of concentration, of planning. She'd do.

The final contestant was a tall black man, in his forties proba-bly. He wore old-fashioned eyeglasses—a mistake. He'd lose them and be seriously handicapped. He kept glancing about with a lopsided grin.

Lottie had finished putting the groceries away; she returned to the living room to sit before the large unit that gave her a better view of the map, above the sectioned screen. The Andes, she had decided, and was surprised and pleased to find she was wrong. Alaska! There were bears and wolves in Alaska still, and elk and moose.

The picture shifted, and a thrill of anticipation raised the hairs on Lottie's arms and scalp. Now the main screen was evenly divided; one half showed the man who had been sliding. He was huddled against the cliff, breathing very hard. On the other half of the screen was an enlarged aerial view. Lottie gasped. Needle-like snow-capped peaks, cliffs, precipices, a rag-ing stream . . . The yellow dot of light that represented the man was on the edge of a steep hill covered with boulders and loose gravel. If he got on that, Lottie thought, he'd be lost. From where he was, there was no way he could know what lay ahead. She leaned forward, examining him for signs that he under-stood, that he was afraid, anything. His face was empty; all he needed now was more air than he could get with his labored breathing.

Andy Stevens stepped in front of the aerial map; it was three feet taller than he. "As you can see, ladies and gentlemen, there is only this scrub growth to Dr. Burnside's left. Those roots might be strong enough to hold, but I'd guess they are shallowly rooted, wouldn't you? And if he chooses this direction, he'll need something to grasp, won't he?" Andy had his tape measure and a pointer. He looked worried. He touched the yellow dot of light. "Here he is. As you can see, he is resting, for the moment, on a narrow ledge after his slide down sixty-five feet of loose dirt and gravel. He doesn't appear to be hurt. Our own Dr. Lederman is watching him along with the rest of us, and he assures me that Dr. Burnside is not injured."

Andy pointed out the hazards of Dr. Burnside's precarious position, and the dangers involved in moving. Lottie nodded, her lips tight and grim. It was off to a good start.

6 P.M. Friday

Butcher got home, as usual, at six. Lottie heard him at the door but didn't get up to open it for him. Dr. Burnside was still sitting there. He had to move. Move, you bastard! Do something!

"Whyn't you unlock the door?" Butcher yelled, yanking off his jacket.

Lottie paid no attention. Butcher always came home mad, resentful because she had got off early, mad at his boss because the warehouse didn't close down early, mad at traffic, mad at everything.

"They say anything about them yet?" Butcher asked, sitting in his recliner.

Lottie shook her head. Move, you bastard! Move!

The man began to inch his way to the left and Lottie's heart thumped, her hands clenched.

"What's the deal?" Butcher asked hoarsely, already responding to Lottie's tension.

"Dead end that way," Lottie muttered, her gaze on the screen. "Slide with boulders and junk if he tries to go down. He's gotta go right."

The man moved cautiously, never lifting his feet from the ground but sliding them along, testing each step. He paused again, this time with less room than before. He looked desperate. He was perspiring heavily. Now he could see the way he had chosen offered little hope of getting down. More slowly than before, he began to back up; dirt and gravel shifted constantly.

The amplifiers picked up the noise of the stuff rushing downward, like a waterfall heard from a distance, and now and then a muttered unintelligible word from the man. The volume came up: he was cursing. Again and again he stopped. He was pale and sweat ran down his face. He didn't move his hands from the cliff to wipe it away.

Lottie was sweating too. Her lips moved occasionally with a faint curse or prayer. Her hands gripped the sofa.

7:30 P.M. Friday

Lottie fell back onto the sofa with a grunt, weak from sustained tension. They were safe. It had taken over an hour to work his way to this place where the cliff and steep slope gave way to a gentle hill. The man was sprawled out face down, his back heaving.

Butcher abruptly got up and went to the bathroom. Lottie couldn't move yet. The screen shifted and the aerial view filled the larger part. Andy pointed out the contestants' lights and finally began the recap.

Lottie watched on the portable set as she got out their frozen dinners and heated the oven. Dr. Lederman was talking about Angie Dawes, the young aspiring actress whose problem was that of having been overprotected all her life. He said she was a potential suicide, and the panel of examining physicians had agreed Crisis Therapy would be helpful.

The next contestant was Mildred Ormsby, a chemist, divorced, no children. She had started on a self-destructive course through drugs, said Dr. Lederman, and would be benefited by Crisis Therapy.

The tall black man, Clyde Williams, was an economist; he taught at Harvard and had tried to murder his wife and their three children by burning down their house with them in it. Crisis Therapy had been indicated.

Finally Dr. Edward Burnside, the man who had started the show with such drama, was shown being interviewed. Forty-one, unmarried, living with a woman, he was a statistician for a major firm. Recently he had started to feed the wrong data into the computer, aware but unable to stop himself.

Dr. Lederman's desk was superimposed on the aerial view and he started his taped explanation of what Crisis Therapy was. Lottie made coffee. When she looked again Eddie was still lying on the ground, exhausted, maybe even crying. She wished he would roll over so she could see if he was crying.

Andy returned to explain how the game was played: the winner received one million dollars, after taxes, and all the contestants were undergoing Crisis Therapy that would enrich their lives beyond measure. Andy explained the automatic, air-cushioned, five-day cameras focused electronically on the contestants, the orbiting satellite that made it possible to keep them under observation at all times, the light amplification, infrared system that would keep them visible all night. This part made Lottie's head ache.

Next came the full-screen commercial for the wall units. Only those who had them could see the entire show. Down the left side of the screen were the four contestants, each in a separate panel, and over them a topographical map that showed the entire region, where the exit points were, the nearest roads, towns. Center screen could be divided any way the director chose. Above this picture was the show's slogan: "This Is Your Crisis!" and a constantly running commercial. In the far right corner there was an aerial view of the selected site, with the colored dots of light. Mildred's was red, Angie's was green. Eddie's yellow, Clyde's blue. Anything else larger than a rabbit or squirrel that moved into the viewing area would be white.

The contestants were shown being taken to the site, first by airplane, then helicopter. They were left there on noon Friday and had until midnight Sunday to reach one of the dozen trucks that ringed the area. The first one to report in at one of the trucks was the winner.

10 P.M. Friday

Lottie made up her bed on the couch while Butcher opened his recliner full length and brought out a blanket and pillow from the bedroom. He had another beer and Lottie drank milk and ate cookies, and presently they turned off the light and there was only the glow from the screen in the room.

The contestants were settled down for the night, each in a sleeping bag, campfires burning low, the long northern twilight still not faded. Andy began to explain the contents of the backpacks.

Lottie closed her eyes, opened them several times, just to check, and finally fell asleep.

1 A.M. Saturday

Lottie sat up suddenly, wide awake, her heart thumping. The red beeper had come on. On center screen the girl was sitting up, staring into darkness, obviously frightened. She must have heard something. Only her dot showed on her screen, but there was no way for her to know that. Lottie lay down again, watching, and became aware of Butcher's heavy snoring. She shook his leg and he shifted and for a few moments breathed deeply, without the snore, then began again.

Francine Dumont was the night M.C.; now she stepped to one side of the screen. "If she panics," Francine said in a hushed voice, "it could be the end of the game for her." She pointed out the hazards in the area—boulders, a steep drop-off, the thickening trees on two sides. "Let's watch," she whispered and stepped back out of the way.

The volume was turned up; there were rustlings in the undergrowth. Lottie closed her eyes and tried to hear them through the girl's ears, and felt only contempt for her. The girl was stiff with fear. She began to build up her campfire. Lottie nodded. She'd stay awake all night, and by late tomorrow she'd be finished. She would be lifted out, the end of Miss Smarty Pants Dawes.

Lottie sniffed and closed her eyes, but now Butcher's snores were louder. If only he didn't sound like a dying man, she thought—sucking in air, holding it, holding it, then suddenly erupting into a loud snort that turned into a gurgle. She pressed her hands over her ears and finally slept again.

2 P.M. Saturday

There were beer cans on the table, on the floor around it. There was half a loaf of bread and a knife with dried mustard and the mustard jar without a top. The salami was drying out, hard, and there were onion skins and bits of brown lettuce and an open jar of pickles. The butter had melted in its dish, and the butter knife was on the floor, spreading a dark stain on the rug.

Nothing was happening on the screen now. Angie Dawes hadn't left the fern patch. She was brushing her hair.

Mildred was following the stream, but it became a waterfall ahead and she would have to think of something else.

The stout man was still making his way downward as directly as possible, obviously convinced it was the fastest way and no more dangerous than any other.

The black man was being logical, like Mildred, Lottie admitted. He watched the shadows and continued in a southeasterly direction, tackling the hurdles as he came to them, methodically, without haste. Ahead of him, invisible to him, but clearly visible to the floating cameras and the audience, were a mother bear and two cubs in a field of blueberries.

Things would pick up again in an hour or so, Lottie knew. Butcher came back. "You have time for a quick shower," Lottie said. He was beginning to smell.

"Shut up." Butcher sprawled in the recliner, his feet bare.

Lottie tried not to see his thick toes, grimy with warehouse dust. She got up and went to the kitchen for a bag, and started to throw the garbage into it. The cans clattered.

"Knock it off, will ya!" Butcher yelled. He stretched to see around her. He was watching the blond braid her hair. Lottie threw another can into the bag.

9 P.M. *Saturday*

Butcher sat on the edge of the chair, biting a fingernail. "See that?" he breathed. "You see it?" He was shiny with perspiration.

Lottie nodded, watching the white dots move on the aerial map, watching the blue dot moving, stopping for a long time, moving again. Clyde and the bears were approaching each other minute by minute, and Clyde knew now that there was something ahead of him.

"You see that?" Butcher cried out hoarsely.

"Just be still, will you?" Lottie said through her teeth. The black man was sniffing the air.

"You can smell a goddam lousy bear a country mile!" Butcher said. "He knows."

"For God's sake, shut up!"

"Yeah, he knows all right," Butcher said softly. "Mother bear, cubs . . . she'll tear him apart."

"Shut up! Shut up!"

Clyde began to back away. He took half a dozen steps, then turned and ran. The bear stood up; behind her the cubs tumbled in play. She turned her head in a listening attitude. She growled and dropped to four feet and began to amble in the direction Clyde had taken. They were about an eighth of a mile apart. Any second she would be able to see him.

Clyde ran faster, heading for thick trees. Past the trees was a cliff he had skirted earlier.

"Saw a cave or something up there," Butcher muttered. "Betcha. Heading for a cave."

Lottie pressed her hands hard over her ears. The bear was closing the gap; the cubs followed erratically, and now and again the mother bear paused to glance at them and growl softly. Clyde began to climb the face of the cliff. The bear came into view and saw him. She ran. Clyde was out of her reach; she began to climb, and rocks were loosened by her great body. When one of the cubs bawled, she let go and half slid, half fell back to the bottom. Standing on her hind legs, she growled at the man above her. She was nine feet tall. She shook her great head from side to side another moment, then turned and waddled back toward the blueberries, trailed by her two cubs.

"Smart bastard," Butcher muttered. "Good thinking. Knew he couldn't outrun a bear. Good thinking."

Lottie went to the bathroom. She had smelled the bear, she thought. If he had only shut up a minute! She was certain she had smelled the bear. Her hands were trembling.

The phone was ringing when she returned to the living room. She answered, watching the screen. Clyde looked shaken, the first time he had been rattled since the beginning.

"Yeah," she said into the phone. "He's here." She put the receiver down. "Your sister."

"She can't come over," Butcher said ominously. "Not unless she's drowned that brat."

"Funny," Lottie said, scowling. Corinne should have enough consideration not to make an issue of it week after week.

"Yeah," Butcher was saying into the phone. "I know it's tough on a floor set, but what the hell, get the old man to buy a wall unit. What's he planning to do, take it with him?" He listened. "Like I said, you know how it is. I say okay, then Lottie gives me hell. Know what I mean? I mean, it ain't worth it. You know?" Presently he banged the receiver down.

"Frank's out of town?"

He didn't answer, settled himself down into his chair and reached for his beer.

"He's in a fancy hotel lobby where they got a unit screen the size of a barn and she's got that lousy little portable . . ."

"Just drop it, will ya? She's the one that wanted the kid, remember. She's bawling her head off but she's not coming over. So drop it!"

"Yeah, and she'll be mad at me for a week, and it takes two to make a kid."

"Jesus Christ!" Butcher got up and went into the kitchen. The refrigerator door banged. "Where's the beer?"

"Under the sink."

"Jesus! Whyn't you put it in the refrigerator?"

"There wasn't enough room for it all. If you've gone through all the cold beers, you don't need any more!"

He slammed the refrigerator door again and came back with a can of beer. When he pulled it open, warm beer spewed halfway across the room. Lottie knew he had done it to make her mad. She ignored him and watched Mildred worm her way down into her sleeping bag. Mildred had the best chance of winning, she thought. She checked her position on the aerial map. All the lights were closer to the trucks now, but there wasn't anything of real importance between Mildred and the goal. She had chosen right every time.

"Ten bucks on yellow," Butcher said suddenly.

"You gotta be kidding! He's going to break his fat neck before he gets out of there!"

"Okay, ten bucks." He slapped ten dollars down on the table, between the TV dinner trays and the coffee pot.

"Throw it away," Lottie said, matching it. "Red."

"The fat lady?"

"Anybody who smells like you better not go around insulting someone who at least takes time out to have a shower now and then!" Lottie cried and swept past him to the kitchen. She and Mildred were about the same size. "And why don't you get off your butt and clean up some of that mess! All I do every weekend is clear away garbage!"

"I don't give a shit if it reaches the ceiling!"

Lottie brought a bag and swept trash into it. When she got near Butcher, she held her nose.

6 A.M. Sunday

Lottie sat up. "What happened?" she cried. The red beeper was on. "How long's it been on?"

"Half an hour. Hell, I don't know."

Butcher was sitting tensely on the side of the recliner, gripping it with both hands. Eddie was in a tree, clutching the trunk. Below him, dogs were tearing apart his backpack, and another dog was leaping repeatedly at him.

"Idiot!" Lottie cried. "Why didn't he hang up his stuff like the others?"

Butcher made a noise at her, and she shook her head, watching. The dogs had smelled food, and they would search for it, tearing up everything they found. She smiled grimly. They might keep Mr. Fat Neck up there all day, and even if he got down, he'd have nothing to eat.

That's what did them in, she thought. Week after week it was the same. They forgot the little things and lost. She leaned back and ran her hand through her hair. It was standing out all over her head.

Two of the dogs began to fight over a scrap of something and the leaping dog jumped into the battle with them. Presently they all ran away, three of them chasing the fourth.

"Throw away your money," Lottie said gaily, and started around Butcher. He swept out his hand and pushed her down again and left the room without a backward look. It didn't matter who won, she thought, shaken by the push. That twenty and twenty more would have to go to the finance company to pay off the loan for the wall unit. Butcher knew that; he shouldn't get so hot about a little joke.

1 P.M. Sunday

"This place looks like a pigpen," Butcher growled. "You going to clear some of this junk away?" He was carrying a sandwich in one hand, beer in the other; the table was littered with breakfast remains, leftover snacks from the morning and the night before.

Lottie didn't look at him. "Clear it yourself."

"I'll clear it." He put his sandwich down on the arm of his chair and swept a spot clean, knocking over glasses and cups.

"Pick that up!" Lottie screamed. "I'm sick and tired of cleaning up after you every damn weekend! All you do is stuff and guzzle and expect me to pick up and clean up."

"Damn right."

Lottie snatched up the beer can he had put on the table and threw it at him. The beer streamed out over the table, chair, over his legs. Butcher threw down the sandwich and grabbed at her. She dodged and backed away from the table into the center of the room. Butcher followed, his hands clenched.

"You touch me again, I'll break your arm!"

"Bitch!" He dived for her and she caught his arm, twisted it savagely and threw him to one side.

He hauled himself up to a crouch and glared at her with hatred. "I'll fix you," he muttered. "I'll fix you!"

Lottie laughed. He charged again, this time knocked her backward and they crashed to the floor together and rolled, pummeling each other.

The red beeper sounded and they pulled apart, not looking at each other, and took their seats before the screen.

"It's the fat lady," Butcher said malevolently. "I hope the bitch kills herself."

Mildred had fallen into the stream and was struggling in waist-high water to regain her footing. The current was very swift, all white water here. She slipped and went under. Lottie held her breath until she appeared again, downstream, retch-ing, clutching at a boulder. Inch by inch she drew herself to it and clung there trying to get her breath back. She looked about desperately; she was very white. Abruptly she launched herself into the current, swimming strongly, fighting to get to the shore as she was swept down the river.

Andy's voice was soft as he said, "That water is forty-eight degrees, ladies and gentlemen! Forty-eight! Dr. Lederman, how long can a person be immersed in water that cold?"

"Not long, Andy. Not long at all." The doctor looked worried too. "Ten minutes at the most, I'd say."

"That water is reducing her body heat second by second," Andy said solemnly. "When it is low enough to produce uncon-sciousness . . ."

Mildred was pulled under again; when she appeared this time, she was much closer to shore. She caught a rock and held on. Now she could stand up, and presently she dragged herself rock by rock, boulder by boulder, to the shore. She was shaking hard, her teeth chattering. She began to build a fire. She could hardly open her waterproof matchbox. Finally she had a blaze and she began to strip. Her backpack, Andy reminded the audi-ence, had been lost when she fell into the water. She had only what she had on her back, and if she wanted to continue after the sun set and the cold evening began, she had to dry her things thoroughly.

"She's got nerve," Butcher said grudgingly.

Lottie nodded. She was weak. She got up, skirted Butcher, and went to the kitchen for a bag. As she cleaned the table, every now and then she glanced at the naked woman by her fire. Steam was rising off her wet clothes.

10 P.M. Sunday

Lottie had moved Butcher's chair to the far side of the table the last time he had left it. His beard was thick and coarse, and he still wore the clothes he had put on to go to work Friday morning. Lottie's stomach hurt. Every weekend she got constipated.

The game was between Mildred and Clyde now. He was in good shape, still had his glasses and his backpack. He was farther from his truck than Mildred was from hers, but she had eaten nothing that afternoon and was limping badly. Her boots must have shrunk, or else she had not waited for them to get completely dry. Her face twisted with pain when she moved.

The girl was still posing in the high meadow, now against a tall tree, now among the wild flowers. Often a frown crossed her face and surreptitiously she scratched. Ticks, Butcher said. Probably full of them.

Eddie was wandering in a daze. He looked empty, and was walking in great aimless circles. Some of them cracked like that, Lottie knew. It had happened before, sometimes to the strongest one of all. They'd slap him right in a hospital and no one would hear anything about him again for a long time, if ever. She didn't waste pity on him.

She would win, Lottie knew. She had studied every kind of wilderness they used and she'd know what to do and how to do it. She was strong, and not afraid of noises. She found herself nodding and stopped, glanced quickly at Butcher to see if he had noticed. He was watching Clyde.

"Smart," Butcher said, his eyes narrowed. "That sonabitch's been saving himself for the home stretch. Look at him." Clyde started to lope, easily, as if aware the TV truck was dead ahead.

Now the screen was divided into three parts, the two finalists, Mildred and Clyde, side by side, and above them a large aerial view that showed their red and blue dots as they approached the trucks.

"It's fixed!" Lottie cried, outraged when Clyde pulled ahead of Mildred. "I hope he falls down and breaks his back!"

"Smart," Butcher said over and over, nodding, and Lottie knew he was imagining himself there, just as she had done. She

felt a chill. He glanced at her and for a moment their eyes held
—naked, scheming. They broke away simultaneously.

Mildred limped forward until it was evident each step was
torture. Finally she sobbed, sank to the ground and buried her
face in her hands.

Clyde ran on. It would take an act of God now to stop him.
He reached the truck at twelve minutes before midnight.

For a long time neither Lottie nor Butcher moved. Neither
spoke. Butcher had turned the audio off as soon as Clyde
reached the truck, and now there were the usual after-game
recaps, the congratulations, the helicopter liftouts of the other
contestants.

Butcher sighed. "One of the better shows," he said. He was
hoarse.

"Yeah. About the best yet."

"Yeah." He sighed again and stood up. "Honey, don't bother
with all this junk now. I'm going to take a shower, and then I'll
help you clean up, okay?"

"It's not that bad," she said. "I'll be done by the time you're
finished. Want a sandwich, doughnut?"

"I don't think so. Be right out." He left. When he came back,
shaved, clean, his wet hair brushed down smoothly, the room
was neat again, the dishes washed and put away.

"Let's go to bed, honey," he said, and put his arm lightly
about her shoulders. "You look beat."

"I am." She slipped her arm about his waist. "We both lost."

"Yeah, I know. Next week."

She nodded. Next week. It was the best money they ever
spent, she thought, undressing. Best thing they ever bought,
even if it would take them fifteen years to pay it off. She yawned
and slipped into bed. They held hands as they drifted off to
sleep.

The Hounds

ROSE ELLEN KNEW that Martin had been laid off, had known it for over a week, but she had waited for him to tell her. She watched him get out of the car on Friday, and she said to herself, "Now he's ready. He's got a plan and he'll tell me what we're going to do, and it'll be all right." There was more relief in her voice, that was in her mind only, than she had thought possible. Why, I've been scared, she thought, in wonder, savoring the feeling now that there was no longer any need to deny it. She knew Martin was ready by the way he left the car. He was a thin intense man, not very tall, five nine. When worried, or preoccupied, or under pressure, he seemed to lose all his coordination. He bumped into furniture, moved jerkily, upsetting things within reach, knocked over coffee cups, glasses. And he forgot to turn things off: water, lights, the car engine once. He had a high domed forehead, thin hair the color of wet sand, and now, after twelve years at the cape, a very deep burned-in suntan. He was driven by a nervous energy that sought release through constant motion. He always had a dozen projects under way: refinishing furniture, assembling a stereo system, designing a space lab model, breeding toy poodles, raising hydroponic vegetables. All his projects turned out well. All were one-man efforts. This afternoon his motion was fluid as he swung his legs out of the car, followed through with a smooth movement, then slammed the door hard. His walk was jaunty as he came up the drive and around the canary date palm to where she waited at the pool-side bar. Rose Ellen was in a bikini, although the air was a bit too cool, and she wouldn't dream of swimming yet. But the sun felt good when the wind died down, and she knew she looked as good in the brief red strips as she had looked fifteen or even twenty years ago. She saw herself reflected in his eyes, not actually, but his expression told her that he was seeing her again. He hadn't for the whole week.

He didn't kiss her; they never kissed until they were going to make love. He patted her bottom and reached for the cocktail shaker. He shook it once then poured and sat down, still looking at her approvingly.

"You know," he said.

"What, honey? I know what?" Her relief put a lilt in her voice, made her want to sing.

"And you've known all along. Well, okay, here's to us."

"Are you going to tell me what it is that I've known all along, or are you just going to sit there looking enigmatic as hell and pleased, and slightly soused?" She leaned over him, looking into his eyes, sniffing. "And how long ago did you leave the office?"

"Noon. Little after. I didn't go back after lunch. I got the can, last Thursday." He put his glass down and pulled her to his lap. "And I don't care."

"May they all rot in hell," Rose Ellen said. "You! You've been there longer than almost anyone. And when they come to you beggin' you to come back, tell them to go to hell. Right?"

"Well, I don't think they'll come begging for me," Martin said, but he was pleased with himself. The worry was gone, and the circles under his eyes seemed less dark, although he still hadn't slept. Rose Ellen pushed herself away from him slightly in order to see him better.

"Anyway, you can get a job up in Jacksonville tomorrow. They know that, don't they? That you'll not be available if they let you go."

"Honey, they aren't Machiavellian, you know. The agency doesn't want to break up our team, but they had no choice, no money, no appropriation for more money. We did what they hired us to do. Now it's over. Let's go to bed."

"Uh-uh! Not until you tell me what's making you grin like that."

"Right. Look, doll, I'm forty-nine. And laid off. You know what the story is for the other guys who've had this happen. No luck. No job. Nothing. It wouldn't be any different with me, honey. You have to accept that."

She kissed his nose and stood up, hands on hips, studying him. "You! You're better than all the others put together. You know you are. You told me yourself a hundred times."

"Honey, I'm forty-nine. No one hires men who are forty-nine."

"Martin, stop this! I won't have it. You're a young man. Educated! My God, you've got degrees nobody ever even heard of. You've got education you've never even used yet."

He laughed and poured his second martini. She knew it pleased him for her to get indignant on his behalf. "I know what I'm talking about, honey. Simmer down, and listen. Okay?" She sat down again, on a stool on the other side of the bar, facing him. A tight feeling had come across her stomach, like the feeling she used to get just before the roller coaster started to go down the last, wildest drop. "I don't want another job, Rose. I've had it with jobs. I want to buy a farm."

She stared at him. He said it again. "We could do it, honey. We could sell the house and with the money left after we pay off the mortgage, the car, the other things, there'd be enough for a small farm. Ten, twenty acres. Not on the coast. Inland. West Virginia. Or Kentucky. I could get a job teaching. I wouldn't mind that."

"Martin? Martin! Stop. It's not funny. It isn't funny at all. Don't go on like this." Her playfulness evaporated leaving only the tight feeling.

"You bet your sweet ass it isn't funny. And I'm serious, Rose. Dead serious."

"A farm! What on earth would I do on the farm? What about the kids?"

"We can work out all those things. . . ."

"Not now, Martin. I have to go get Juliette. Later, later." She ran into the house without looking back at him. Bad strategy, she thought at herself dressing. She should have gone to bed with him, and then talked him out of his crazy notion. That's all it was, a crazy notion. He was as scared as she was. He could get a job in Jacksonville. He could. It wasn't a bad drive. He could come home weekends, if he didn't want to drive it every day, although some people did. She thought about the house payments, and the insurance, and the pool maintenance, and the yard people, and the housecleaning woman who came twice a week. And the lessons: piano, ballet, scuba, sailing. The clubs. The marina where they left the ketch. She thought of her dressmaker and her hairdresser, and his tailor, and the special shoes for Annamarie, and the kennel fees when they went away for the weekend and had to leave the three toy poodles. She thought of two thousand dollars worth of braces for Juliette in another two years.

She thought about the others it had happened to. Out of six close friends only one, Burdorf, had another job, advisor to an ad agency. But Burdorf had an in with them; his wife's father owned it.

Rose Ellen tried to stop thinking of the others who had been laid off. But Martin was different, she thought again. Really different. He had so many degrees, for one thing. She shook her head. That didn't matter. It hadn't mattered for any of the others.

She thought about being without him. She and the children

without him. She shivered and hugged herself hard. She could go to work. She hadn't because neither of them had wanted her to before. But she could. She could teach, actually, easier than Martin could. He didn't have any of the education courses that were required now. So, she pursued it further, she would teach, at about seven thousand a year, and Martin would have to pay, oh, say four hundred a month. . . . And if he didn't, or couldn't? If he was on a farm somewhere without any money at all? Seven thousand. Braces, two thousand. House, two thousand. Some extras, not many, but some, like a car. In another year Annamarie would be driving, and junior insurance, and then Jeffrey would be wanting a car. . . .

More important, they wouldn't mind her. She knew it. Martin could control them with a word, a glower. She was easy and soft with them. It had always been impossible to tell them no, to tell them she wouldn't take them here or there, do this or that for them. They'd run all over her, she knew.

Martin bought a farm in May and they moved as soon as school was out. The farm was twelve acres, with a small orchard and a deep well and barn. The house was modern and good, and the children, surprisingly, accepted the move unquestioningly and even liked it all. They held a family council the day after moving into the house and took a vote on whether to buy a pool table for the basement rec room, or a horse. It would be the only luxury they could afford for a long time. Only Rose Ellen voted for the pool table.

Martin had to take three courses at the university in the fall semester, then he would teach, starting in mid-term, not his own field of mathematics, because they had a very good teacher already, he was told, but if he could brush up on high school general science. . . .

Rose Ellen signed up as a substitute teacher for the fall semester. The school was only a mile and a half from their house, she could walk there when the weather was pleasant.

"It's going to be all right, honey," Martin said one night in early September. Everyone had started school, the whole move to the country had been so without trauma that it was suspicious. Rose Ellen nodded, staring at him. "What's wrong?" he asked. "Dirt on my face?"

"No. It's strange how much you looked like my father there for a moment. A passing expression, there and gone so fast that I probably imagined it."

"Your father?"

She picked up the magazine she had been looking at. "Yes. I told you I couldn't remember him because I didn't want to talk about him. It was a lie. He didn't die until I was eleven."

Martin didn't say anything, and reluctantly she lowered the magazine again. "I'm sorry. But after I told you that, back in the beginning, I was stuck with it. I'm glad it came out finally."

"Do you want to talk about him?"

"No. Not really. He drank a lot. He and mother fought like animals most of the time. Then he died in a car accident. Drunk driving, hit a truck head on, killed himself, nearly killed the driver of the truck. Period. When I was fourteen she married again, and this time it was to a rich man."

"Did she love Eddie?"

"Eddie was the practical one," Rose Ellen said. "She married for love the first time, for practical reasons the second time. The second one was better. They've been peaceful together. No more fights. No more dodging bill collectors. Like that."

"Did she love him?"

"I don't know. I don't think so, but it didn't matter."

Martin didn't say any more, and she wondered about her mother and her second husband. Had it mattered? She didn't know. She turned pages of the magazine without looking at them, and Martin's voice startled her.

"Sometimes I think we should fight now and then," he said. "I wonder sometimes what all you're bottling up."

"Me? You know we discuss everything."

"Discuss isn't what I mean. We discuss only after you get quiet and stay quiet long enough to come to a decision. I'd like to know sometimes what all goes on in that head of yours while you're in the process of deciding."

She laughed and stood up. "Right now all that's in my head is the fact that I want a bath and bed."

She was at the door to the kitchen when Martin asked, "What did your father do?"

She stopped. Without turning around again she said, "He had a small farm. Nothing else."

She soaked for a while and thought about his words. It was true that they never fought. He hadn't lived with two people who did fight, or he'd never say anything like that. She knew it was better to be civilized and give in. She was a good wife, she told herself soberly. A good wife. And she was adaptable. He had taken her from Atlanta to Florida, from there to Kentucky. So be it. She could get along no matter where they lived, or what they did. One of them had to, she said sharply in her mind. She had been a silent observer in her own house, then in her step-father's house for years. It was better that way. She let the water out and rubbed herself briskly. At the bathroom door she saw that Martin had come up, their light was on. She paused for a few seconds, then went downstairs to read. She had been more tired than sleepy, she decided. Actually it was quite early.

October was still days of gold and red light, of blue skies that were endlessly deep, of russet leaves underfoot and flaming maples and scarlet poison ivy and sumac, yellow poplars and ash trees. She walked home from school with a shopping bag under her arm, alone on the narrow road that was seldom used, except by the half dozen families that lived along it. Here one side was bordered by a fence line long grown up with blackberries and boysenberries and inhabited by small scurrying things that were invisible. The other side had a woods, not very dense, then a field of corn that had been harvested so that only skeletons remained. Behind the fence line was a pasture with a stream, peaceful cows that never once looked up as she passed them. The pasture ended, a stand of pine trees came up to the road. Then there was an outcropping of limestone and a hill with oak trees and some tall firs, and walnut trees. Walnuts had dropped over the road, along both sides of it.

She stopped at the walnuts and began to gather the heavy green hulls, hardly even broken by the fall. They would have to spread them out, let them dry. A scene from her childhood came to her, surprising her. There were so few scenes from her early years that sometimes she worried about it. They had gathered nuts one day. She, her mother, her father, out along a dirt road near their farm, gathering hickory nuts, and butternuts. They had taken a lunch with them, and had eaten it by a stream, and she had waded, although the water had been icy. Her father had made a fire and she had warmed her feet at it. She saw again his smiling face looking up at her as he rubbed her cold toes between his warm hands.

She finished filling her bag and picked up her purse again. Then she saw the dogs. Two of them stood on the other side of the road, behind the single strand of wire that was a fence. They were silver, and long legged, and very beautiful. They were as motionless as statues. She moved and their eyes followed her; they remained motionless. Their eyes were large, like deers' eyes, and golden. She turned to look at them again after passing them; they were watching her.

That night she tried to describe them to Martin. "Hunting dogs, I'd guess," she said. "But I've never seen any like them before. They were as skinny as possible to still have enough muscles to stand up with. All long muscles and bones, and that amazing silver hair."

Martin was polite, but not really interested, and she became silent about them. The children were upstairs in their rooms, studying. She realized that she saw very little of them any more. They had adapted so well that they were busy most of the time, and the school days here were longer, the buses were later than they used to be, so that they didn't get home until four-fifteen. Then there were the things that teen-agers always did: telephone; records; riding the horse, currying it, feeding it; Jeffrey out on his bike with other boys. . . . She sighed and began to look over the papers she had brought home to grade. She would have Miss Witner's fifth-grade class for another week. She decided that she detested geography.

The next afternoon the dogs were there again; this time they left the field as she came near, and stood just off the road while she passed them. She spoke to them in what she hoped was a soothing voice, but they seemed not to hear; they merely stared at her.

They were bigger than she had remembered. Their tails were like silver plumes, responding to the gentle breeze as delicately as strands of silk. Feathery silver hair stirred on their chests and the backs of their long, thin legs.

She slowed down, but continued to walk evenly until she was past them, then she looked back; they were watching her.

Her father had had a hound dog, she remembered suddenly. And her mother had let it loose one day. They never had found it. Sometimes at night she had thought she could hear its strange voice from the hills. It had a broken howl that distinguished it from the other hounds. It started high, rose and rose, then broke and started again on a different key.

She never had wondered why her mother let it go, but now she did. How furious her father had been. They had screamed at each other for hours, and just as suddenly they had been laughing at each other, and that had been all of the scene. She realized that they had gone to bed, that they always had gone to bed after one of their fights. Everything they had done together had been like that, fierce, wild, uninhibited, thorough. And now her mother was growing old in Eddie's fine house, with no one to yell at, no one to yell at her. No one to make up with. Rose Ellen resisted the impulse to look back at the dogs.

She knew they would be watching her. She didn't want to see them watching her again.

The next day was Friday and she left school later than usual, after a short staff meeting about a football game. As a substitute she didn't have to attend the meeting, and certainly she wasn't required to go to the game, but she thought she might. If Jeffrey wanted to go, she would take him. Maybe they would all go. The sun was low and the afternoon was cooler than it had been all week. She walked fast, then stopped. The dogs were there. Suddenly she was terrified. And she felt stupid. They were polite, well-behaved dogs, very valuable from the looks of them. They must belong to John Renfrew. They were always at his property line anyway. She wondered if he knew they were loose. Or were they so well trained that they wouldn't leave his property? She started to move ahead again, but slowly. When she got even with them, they moved too. Not at her side, but a step behind her. She stopped and they stopped and looked at her.

"Scat," she said. "Go home." They stared at her. "Go on home!" She felt a mounting fear and shook it off with annoyance. They weren't menacing or frightening, not growling, or making any threatening movement at all. They were merely dumb. She pointed toward John Renfrew's field again. "Go home!" They watched her.

She started to walk again, and they accompanied her home. She couldn't make them go back, or stop, or sit, or anything. No matter what she said, they simply looked at her. She wondered if they were deaf and mute, and decided that she was being silly now. They would have followed her inside the house if she hadn't closed the door before they could.

"Martin!" The three champagne-colored poodles were ecstatic over her return. They jumped on her, and pranced, and got in the way, yapping. She hadn't noticed the car, but he could have put it in the garage, she thought, looking in the study, the kitchen, opening the basement door, stepping over poodles automatically. No one else was home yet. She looked out the window. They were sitting on the porch, waiting for her. She pulled back and found that she was shivering.

"This is ridiculous!" she said. "They are dogs!" She looked up Renfrew's number and called him. His wife answered.

"Who? Oh, yes. I've been meaning to come over there, but we've been so busy. You understand."

"Yes. Yes. But I'm afraid your dogs followed me home today. I tried to make them go back, but they wouldn't."

"Dogs? You mean Lucky? I thought I saw him a minute ago. Yes, he's here. I can see him out in the yard."

"These are hunting dogs. They are silver colored, long tails . . ."

"Our Lucky is a border collie. Black and white. And he's home. I don't know whose dogs you have, but not ours. We don't have any hunting dogs."

Rose Ellen hung up. She knew they were still there. The back door slammed and Jeffrey and Annamarie were home. Presently Juliette would be there, and Martin would be back, and they could all decide what to do about the dogs on the porch. Rose Ellen went to the kitchen, ready to make sandwiches, or start dinner, or anything. She felt a grim satisfaction that she had successfully resisted looking at the dogs again. Let them wait, she thought.

"Hi, kids. Hungry?"

"Hi, Mom. Can I stay over at Jennifer's house tonight? She's a drum majorette and has to go to the game, and I thought I might go too, with Frank and Sue Cox, and then go to Jennifer's house for hamburgers and cokes after?"

Rose Ellen blinked at Annamarie. "I suppose so," she said. Jennifer was the daughter of the principal. She marveled at how quickly children made friends.

"I have to run, then," Annamarie said. "I have to get some pants on, and my heavy sweater. Do you think I'll need a jacket? Did you hear the weather? How cold will it get?" But she was running upstairs as she talked, and out of earshot already.

"Well, how about you?" Rose Ellen said to Jeffrey. "You going to the game too?"

"Yeah. We're ushers. That's our chore, you know. This month we do that, then we sell candy at the basketball games after Christmas. Is it okay if I have a hot dog and go? I told Mike I'd meet him at his house, and we'll catch the bus there."

Rose Ellen nodded. Martin and Juliette came home together then. He had picked her up at the bus stop.

They had dinner, and Juliette vanished to make one of her interminable phone calls to Betsy, her all-time closest friend. Rose Ellen told Martin about the dogs. "They're out on the porch," she said. "I'm sure they're very expensive. No collars."

With the three toy poodles dancing around him, Martin went to the door to look. The hounds walked in when the door opened. The poodles drew back in alarm; they sniffed the big dogs, and then ignored them. Rose Ellen felt tight in her stomach. The silly poodles were always panicked by another dog.

"Good God," Martin said. "They're beautiful!" He clicked his fingers and called softly, "Come on, boy. Come here." The dogs seemed oblivious of him. They looked at Rose Ellen. Martin walked around them, then reached down tentatively and put his hand on the nearer one's head. The dog didn't move. He ran his hand over the shoulders, down the flank, down the leg. The dog didn't seem to notice. Martin felt both dogs the same way. He ran his hand over the shoulders, down the lean sides of the dogs, over their bellies, again and again. A strange look came over his face and abruptly he pulled away. "Have you felt them?"

"No."

"You should. It's like silk. Warm and soft and alive under your fingers. My god, it's the most sensuous dog I've ever seen." He backed off and studied them both. They continued to watch Rose Ellen. "Come on and feel them. You can see how tame they are."

She shook her head. "Put them out, Martin."

"Rose? What's wrong with you? Are you afraid of them? You've never been afraid of dogs before. The poodles . . ."

"They're not dogs. They're animated toys. And I have always been afraid of dogs. Put them out!" Her voice rose slightly. Martin went to the door, calling the dogs. They didn't move. She had known they wouldn't. Slowly she walked to the door. They followed her. Martin watched, puzzled. She walked out on the porch, and the dogs went too. Then she went back inside, opening the door only enough to slip in, not letting them come with her. They sat down and waited.

"Well, they know who they like," Martin said. "You must be imprinted on their brains, like a duckling imprints what he sees first and thinks it's his mother." He laughed and went back to the table for his coffee.

Rose Ellen was cold. She wasn't afraid, she told herself. They were the quietest, most polite dogs she had ever seen. They were the least threatening dogs she had ever seen. Probably the most expensive ones she had ever seen. Still she was very cold.

"What will we do about them?" she asked, holding her hot coffee cup with both hands, not looking at Martin.

"Oh, advertise, I guess. The owner might have an ad in the paper, in fact. Have you looked?"

She hadn't thought of it. They looked together, but there was nothing. "Okay, tomorrow I'll put in an ad. Probably there'll be a reward. Could be they got away miles from here, over near Lexington. I'll put an ad in Lexington papers, too."

"But what will we do with them until the owner comes to get them?"

"What can we do? I'll feed them and let them sleep in the barn."

Even the coffee cup in her hands couldn't warm her. She thought of the gold eyes watching all night, waiting for her to come out.

"Honey, are you all right?"

"Yes. Of course. I just think they're . . . strange, I guess. I don't like them."

"That's because you didn't feel them. You should have. I've never felt anything like it."

She looked at her cup. She knew there was no power on earth that could induce her to touch one of those dogs.

Rose Ellen woke up during the night. The dogs, she thought. They were out there waiting for her. She tried to go to sleep again, but she was tense and every time she closed her eyes she saw the gold eyes looking at her. Finally she got up. She couldn't see the porch from her bedroom, but from Juliette's room she could. She covered Juliette, as if that was what she had entered the room for, then she started to leave resolutely. It was crazy to go looking for them, as crazy as it was for them to keep watching her. At the hall door she stopped, and finally she turned and went back to the window. They were there.

The hall night light shone dimly on the porch, and in the square of soft light the two animals were curled up with the head of one of them on the back of the other. As she looked at them they both raised their heads and looked up at her, their eyes gleaming gold. She stifled a scream and dropped the curtain, shaking.

On Saturday morning, Joe MacLaughton, the county agent, came over to help Martin plan for a pond that he wanted to have dug. He looked at the dogs admiringly. "You sure have a pair of beauties," he said. "You don't want to let them loose in those hills. Someone'll sure as hell lift them."

"I wish they would," Rose Ellen said. She was tired; she hadn't slept after going back to bed at three-thirty.

"Ma'am?" Joe said politely.

"They aren't ours. They followed me home."

"You don't say?" He walked around the dogs thoughtfully. "They don't come from around here," he said finally.

"I'm going to call the paper and put an ad in the Lost and Found," Martin said.

"Waste of time in the locals," Joe said stubbornly. "If those dogs belonged around here, I'd know about it. Might try the kennel club over in Lexington, though."

Martin nodded. "That's a thought. They must know about such valuable dogs in this area."

They went out to look at the proposed pond site. The dogs stayed on the porch, looking at the door.

After the agent left, Martin made his calls. The kennel club president was no help. Weimaraners? Martin said no, and he named another breed or two, and then said he'd have to have a look at the dogs, didn't sound like anything he knew. After he hung up, Martin swore. He had an address in Lexington where he could take the dogs for identification. He called the newspaper and placed the ad.

All day the sound of hammering from the barn where Martin was making repairs sounded and resounded. Annamarie and Jennifer came in and volunteered to gather apples. Jeffrey helped his father, and Juliette tagged with one pair, then the other. She tried to get the dogs to play with her, but they wouldn't. After patting them for a few minutes she ignored them as thoroughly as they ignored all the children. Rose didn't go outside all day. She started to leave by the back door once, but they heard her and walked around the corner of the house before she got off the steps. She returned to the kitchen. They returned to the porch.

They wouldn't stay in the barn. There were too many places where creatures as thin as they were could slip through, so Martin didn't even try to make them stay there. They seemed to prefer the porch. No one wanted to go to town to buy collars for them in order to tie them up. Martin didn't like the idea of tying them up anyway. "What if they decide to go back to where they came from?" he asked. Rose didn't press the idea after that.

At dinner she said, "Let's go over to Lexington to a movie tonight?"

Martin sagged. "What's playing?"

She shrugged. "I don't know. Something must be playing that we'd like to see."

"Another night? Tomorrow night?" Martin said. "Tell you what, I'll even throw in dinner."

"Oh, never mind. It was a sudden thought. I don't even know what's on." Rose and Annamarie cleared the table and she brought in apple pie, and coffee. She thought of the dogs on the porch.

"Next February I'll spray the trees," Martin said. "And I'll fertilize under the trees. Watch and see the difference then. Just wait."

Rose Ellen nodded. Just wait. Martin was tired, and thinner than usual. He worked harder here than he ever had anywhere, she was sure. Building, repairing, planting, studying about farming methods, and his school courses. She wondered if he was happy. Later, she thought, later she would ask him if he was happy. She wondered if that was one of those questions that you don't ask unless you already know the answer. Would she dare ask if she suspected that he might answer no? She hoped he wouldn't ask her.

Martin was an inventive lover. It pleased him immensely to delight her, or give her an unexpected thrill, or just to stay with her for an hour. They made love that night and afterward, both drowsy and contented, she asked if he was happy.

"Yes," he said simply. And that was that. "I wish you were, too," he said moments later. She had almost fallen asleep. She stiffened at his words. "Sorry, honey. Relax again. Okay?"

"What did you mean by that?"

"I'm not sure. Sometimes I just feel that I've got it all. You, the kids, the farm now, and school. I can't think of anything else I want."

"I've got all those things too, you know."

"I know." He stretched and yawned and wanted to let it drop.

"Martin, you must have meant something. You think I'm not happy, is that it?"

"I don't know. I don't know what it takes to make you happy."

She didn't reply and soon he was asleep. She didn't know either.

She dozed after a while, and was awakened by a rhythmic noise that seemed to start in her dream, then linger after the dream faded. She turned over, but the noise didn't go away. She turned again and snuggled close to Martin. The bedroom was chilly. A wind had started to blow, and the window was open too much. She felt the air current on her cheek, and finally got up to close the window. The noise was louder. She got her robe on and went into the hall, then to the window in Juliette's room. The dogs were walking back and forth on the porch, their nails clicking with each step. They both stopped and looked at her. She ran from the room shaking, and strangely, weeping.

At breakfast she said to Martin, "You have to get them out of here today. I can't stand them any longer."

"They really got to you, didn't they?"

"Yes, they got to me! Take them to Lexington, leave them with the kennel club people, or the dog pound, or something."

"Okay, Rose. Let's wait until afternoon. See if anyone answers our ad first."

No one called about them, and at one Martin tried to get them into the car. They refused to leave the porch. "I could carry them," he said, doubtfully. They weren't heavy, obviously. Anything as thin as they couldn't be heavy. But when he tried to lift one, it started to shiver, and it struggled and slipped through his arms. When he tried again, the dog growled, a hoarse sound of warning deep in its throat, not so much a threat as a plea not to make it follow through. Its gold eyes were soft and clear and very large. Martin stopped. "Now what?" he asked.

"I'll get them to the car," Rose said. She led the two dogs to the car and opened the door for them. They jumped inside. When she closed the door again, they pressed their noses against the window and looked at her. "See if they'll let you drive," she said.

They wouldn't let Martin get inside the car at all, not until Rose was behind the wheel, and then they paid no attention to him. "I'll drive," she said tightly. Her hands on the wheel were very stiff and the hard feeling in her stomach made it difficult to breathe. Martin nodded. He reached out and put his hand on her knee and squeezed it gently.

He was saying it was all right, but it wasn't, she thought, driving.

The kennel club was run by Colonel Owen Luce, who was a Kentucky colonel, and wanted the title used. "Proud of it, you know," he said genially. "Got mine the hard way, through service. Nowadays you can buy it, but not back when I got mine." He was forty, with blond wavy hair, tall and too good looking not to know it. He posed and swaggered and preened, and reminded Rose of a peacock that had stolen bread from their picnic table at Sunken Gardens in Florida once.

"They're handsome dogs," Colonel Luce said, walking around the hounds. "Handsome. Deer hounds? No. Not with that silky hair. Hm. Don't tell me. Not wolf hounds. Got it! Salukis!" He looked at Rose, waiting for approval. She shrugged. "I'm not certain," he said, as if by admitting his fallibility, he was letting her in on a closely guarded secret that very few would ever know. He didn't ignore Martin as much as by-pass him, first glancing at him, then addressing himself to Rose. Obviously he thought she was the dog fancier, since the hounds clung to her so closely.

"We don't know what they are," she said. "And they aren't ours. They followed me home. We want to return them to their owner."

"Ah. You should get quite a reward then. There aren't many salukis in this country. Very rare, and very expensive."

"We don't want a reward," Rose said. "We want to get rid of them."

"Why? Are they mean?" It was a ridiculous question. He smiled to show he was joking. "I always heard that salukis were more nervous than these seem to be," he said, studying them once more. "And the eyes are wrong, I think, if memory serves. I wonder if they could be a cross?"

Rose looked at Martin imploringly, but he was looking stubborn. He disliked the colonel very much. "Colonel Luce, can you house these dogs?" Rose asked. "You can claim the reward, and if no one shows up to claim them, then they'd be yours by default, wouldn't they? You could sell them."

"My dear lady, I couldn't possibly. We don't know anything about a medical history for them, now do we? I would have to assume that they've had nothing in the way of shots, obviously not true, but with no records." He spread his hands and smiled prettily at Rose. "You do understand. I would have to isolate them for three weeks, to protect my own dogs. And give them the shots, and the examinations, and then have an irate owner show up? No thank you. Owners of valuable dogs tend to get very nasty if you doctor their hounds for them without their approval."

"Christ!" Martin said in disgust. "How much would you charge to board them then?"

"In isolation? Eight dollars a day, each."

Rose stared at him. He smiled again, showing every tooth in his head. She turned away. "Let's go, Martin." She took the dogs to the car and opened the door for them. She got behind the wheel and Martin got in, and only then did the dogs sit down. The dog pound was closed. "They won't get in the car again," Rose said dully. "Can you think of any place else?" He couldn't and she started for home.

The blue grass country that they drove through was very lovely at that time of year. The fields rose and fell gently, delineated by white fences, punctuated in the distance by dark horses. Stands of woods were bouquets in full bloom, brilliant in the late afternoon sunlight. A haze softened the clear blue of the sky, and in the far distance hazy blue hills held the sky and land apart. Rose looked at it all, then said bitterly, "I shouldn't have let you do this."

"What?"

"Come here. Bring me here."

"Honey, what's wrong? Don't you like the farm?"

"I don't know. I just know I should have told you no. We should have tried to work it out without this."

"Rose, you didn't say anything about not wanting to come here. Not a word."

"You might have known, if you hadn't closed your eyes to what I wanted. You always close your eyes to what I want. It's always what you want. Always."

"That isn't fair. How in God's name was I supposed to know what you were thinking? You didn't say anything. You knew we had to do something. We couldn't keep the house and the boat and everything, we had to do something."

"You didn't even try to get a job!"

"Rose. Don't do this now. Wait until we get home."

She slowed down. "Sorry. But, Martin, it's like that with us. You say you want to do this or that, and we do it. Period. It's always been like that with us. I never had a voice in anything."

"You never spoke out."

"You wouldn't let me! It was always decided first, then you told me. You always just assumed that if you wanted something then I would too. As if I exist only in your shadow, as if I must want what you want without fail, without question."

"Rose, I never thought that. If I made the decisions it was only because you wouldn't. I don't know how many times I've brought something up for us to talk about and decide on, only to have you too busy, or not interested, or playing helpless."

"Playing helpless? What's that supposed to mean? You mean when you tell me we're moving I should chain myself to a tree and say no? Is that how I could have a voice? What can I do when you say we're doing this and you have the tickets, the plans, the whole thing worked out from beginning to end? When have you ever said how about doing this, before you already had it all arranged?"

He was silent and she realized that she had been speeding

again. She slowed down. "I didn't want children right away. But
you did. Bang, children. I didn't want to move to Florida, but
you had such a great job there. What a great job! Bang, we're
in Florida. I might have been a teacher. Or a success in business.
Or something. But no, I had to have children and stay home and
cook and clean and look pretty for you and your friends."

"Rose." Martin's voice was low. He looked straight ahead.
"Rose, please stop now. I didn't realize how much of this you
had pent up. But not now. Or let me drive. Pull off the road."

She hit the brakes hard, frightened suddenly. Her hands were
shaking. She saw the dogs in the rear view mirror. "They
wouldn't let you drive," she said. "Will you light me a cigarette,
please?"

He gave it to her wordlessly, staring ahead. She reached for
the radio and he said, "Let me do it." He tuned in country music
and she reached for it again. He changed the station to a press
interview with someone from HEW.

Rose stubbed the cigarette out. "Martin, I'm frightened.
We've never done that before. Not in the car anyway, not like
that."

"I know," he said. He still didn't look at her.

She drove slowly and carefully the last ten minutes and neither of them spoke again until they were inside the house, the
dogs on the porch. "Why'd you bring them back?" Jeffrey asked
disgustedly. He thought that dogs as big as they were should be
willing to retrieve, or something.

Martin told them about the colonel and Rose went upstairs to
wash her face and hands. Halfway up the stairs, she turned and
called, "Martin will you put some coffee on, please." And he
answered cheerfully.

It was the dogs, she told herself in the bathroom. They had
made the quarrel happen, somehow. She couldn't really remember what they had quarreled about, only that it had been
ugly and dangerous. Once when she had glanced at the speed-
ometer, it had registered eighty-five. She shivered thinking of

it. It had been the dogs' fault, she knew, without being able to think how they had done it, or why, or what the argument had been about.

Annamarie had made potato salad, and they had ham with it, and baked apples with heavy cream for dessert. Throughout dinner Rose was aware of Martin's searching gaze on her, and although she smiled at him, he didn't respond with his own wide grin, but remained watchful and quiet.

After the children went to bed, Martin wanted to talk about it, but she wouldn't. "Not now," she said. "I have to think. I don't know what happened, and I have to think."

"Rose, we can't just leave it at that. You said some things I never had thought of before. I had no idea you felt left out of our decisions. I honestly believed you wanted it like that."

She put her hands over her ears. "Not now! Please, Martin, not now. I have to think."

"And then hit me with it again, that I don't talk things over with you?"

"Shut up! Can't you for the love of God just shut up?"

He stared at her and she took a deep breath, but didn't soften it at all. "Sure," he said. "For now."

That night she finally fell asleep breathing in time to the clicking of the dogs' nails on the porch floor. She dreamed. She floated downstairs with a long pale silk negligee drifting around her, like a bride of Dracula. She could see herself, a faint smile on her lips, her hair long and loose. It didn't look very much like her, but that was unimportant. The air was pleasantly cool on her skin, and she glided across the yard, beckoning to her dogs to come. There was a moon that turned everything into white and black and gray and the world now was not the same one that she had known before. Her horse was waiting for her and she floated up to mount it. Then they were flying across the fields, she on the horse, the dogs at one side. They were painfully beautiful running, their silver hair blowing; stretched out they seemed not to touch the ground at all. They looked like silver light flowing above the ground. Her horse ran easily, silently, and there was no sound at all in this new world. The field gave way to the forest where the light from the moon came down in silver shafts, aslant and gleaming. The dogs disappeared in the shadows, appeared, dazzling bright in the moonlight, only to vanish again. They ran and ran, without a sound and she had no fear of hitting anything. Her horse knew its way. They reached the end of the motionless woods, and there was a meadow sprinkled with spiderwebs that were like fine lace glistening with dew that caught the moonlight like pearls. They slowed down now. Somewhere ahead was the game that they chased. Now the dogs were fearful to her. The golden eyes gleamed and they became hunting machines. First one, then the other sniffed the still air, and then with a flicker of motion they were off again, her horse following, not able to keep up with them. They were on the trail. She saw the deer then, a magnificent buck with wide spread antlers. It saw the dogs and leaped through the air, twenty feet, thirty feet, an impossible leap executed in slow motion. But the dogs had it, and she knew it, and the buck knew it. It ran from necessity; it was the prey, they the hunters, and the ritual forced it to run. She stopped to watch the kill, and this was as silent as the entire hunt had been. The dogs leaped and the deer fell and presently the dogs drew away from it, bloody now, and stood silently watching her.

She woke up. She was shivering as if with fever.

Martin took her to school, and when she got out of the car, he said, "I'll be back before you're through. I'll pick you up." She nodded. The dogs were on the porch when they got home that afternoon.

That night he asked her if she was ready to talk. She looked at him helplessly. "I don't know. I can't think of anything to say."

"How about what's bugging you?"

"The dogs. Nothing else."

"Not the dogs."

"That's all, Martin. They're haunting me."

"Live dogs can't haunt anyone." He picked up his book and began to make notes.

Tuesday he met her after school again. The dogs were on the porch when they got home. She didn't look at them.

On Wednesday Martin had a late class and wouldn't be home until after six. "Will you be all right?" he asked, when he dropped her off.

"Yes. Of course."

He reached for her arm, and holding it, looked at her for a moment. He let her go. "Right. See you later."

When she turned into the county road after school the dogs were there waiting for her. She felt dizzy and faint, and stopped, steadying herself with one hand on a tree. She looked back toward the school, a quarter of a mile down the highway. She shook her head. Stupid! Stupid! She started to walk, trying not to look at the golden eyes that watched her. For three nights they had shared a common dream, and she felt suddenly that they knew about it, and that was the link that bound them together. She walked too fast and began to feel winded and hot. It was as quiet on the little road as it was in the fields and woods of her dream. No wind blew, no leaves stirred, even the birds were silent. She picked up a stick, and looked quickly at the dogs, slightly behind her, so that in order to see them she had to turn her head slightly. They trotted silently, watching her.

Each night in the dream she got closer to the deer before the kill, and that night she was afoot, standing close enough to touch it when the dogs leaped. In her hand was a knife, and when the dogs felled the animal, she braced herself to leap also.

"No!" She sat up throwing off the covers, thrashing about frantically, moaning now. Martin caught her and held her still until she was wide awake.

"Honey, you've got to tell me. Please, Rose. Please."

"I can't," she moaned. "It's gone now. A nightmare."

He didn't believe her, but he held her and stroked her hair and made soothing noises. "I love you," he said over and over. "I love you. I love you."

And finally she relaxed and found that she was weeping. "I love you, Martin," she said, sobbing suddenly. "I do. I really do."

"I know you do," he said. "I'm glad that you know it too."

On Thursday she learned that the teacher she was subbing for was well and would return the following day. Martin picked her up after school and she told him.

"I don't want you to stay home all day with those dogs," he said. "I'll get them in the car somehow and take them to the pound. No one is going to claim them."

She shook her head. "You can't," she said.

"I can try."

But he couldn't. They refused to budge from the porch on Friday morning. Rose watched from inside the house. She hadn't slept at all during the night. She had been afraid to, and she felt dopey and heavy limbed. All night she had sat up watching television, drinking coffee, eating cheese and apples and cookies, reading. Listening to the clicking nails on the porch.

"I'll stay home, then," Martin said when they both knew that the dogs were not going to go with him. "Or, maybe you could trick them into getting in the car."

But they knew she couldn't. The dogs wouldn't move for her either. He approached them with the idea of trying to carry them, and they both growled, and the hairs on their necks bristled.

"Martin, just go. We'll have all weekend to decide what to do with them. They'll sit out there and I'll stay in here. It's all right. You'll be late."

He kissed her then, and she felt surprise. He never kissed her when he left. Only when they were going to go to bed, or were in bed already. "Stay inside. Promise?"

She nodded and watched him drive away. The dogs looked at her. "What do you want from me?" she demanded, going out

to the porch, standing before them. "Just what do you want?"
She took a step toward them. *"What do you want?"* She realized that the screaming voice was her own and she stopped. She
was very near them now. She could touch them if she reached
out. They waited for her to touch them, to stroke them. Suddenly she whirled around and ran back inside the house. They
didn't try to get in this time. They knew she would be back.

She went to the kitchen feeling dull and blank and heavy. She
poured coffee and sat down at the kitchen table with it, and
then put her head down on her arms. Drifting, drifting, the
warmth of sleep stealing over her. Suddenly she jumped up,
knocking over her coffee. No! She knew she must not sleep,
must not dream that dream again. She made more coffee and
cleaned up the mess she had made, then washed the dishes. She
put clothes in the washer, made the beds, peeled apples to
make jelly, and all the time the clicking back and forth went on.
She turned on the radio, and found herself listening over the
music for the noise of their nails. She turned it off again. At noon
she looked at them from Juliette's room. They turned to watch
her, stopping in their tracks when she lifted the curtain. The
light caught in the gold eyes, making them look as if they were
flashing at her. Signals flashing at her. She let the curtain fall and
backed away.

Then she went to Martin's study and took down his rifle. She
loaded it carefully and walked out the back door, letting it slam
behind her. She didn't turn to see if they were coming. She
knew they were. At the back of the barn she waited for them.
She thought of how beautiful they were running, how silky and
fine their hair was, alive and blowing in the wind. They came
around the corner of the barn, walking quietly, very sure of her.
She raised the rifle, aiming it carefully, as Martin had taught
her. The large gold eyes caught the sun and flashed. She shot.
The first dog dropped without a whimper. The other one was
transfixed. He hadn't believed she would do it. Neither of them
had believed her capable of doing it. She aimed again and shot.

She was looking into the golden eyes as she pulled the trigger. She saw the light go out in them.

She dropped the rifle and hid her face in her hands. She was shaking violently. Then she vomited repeatedly and after there was nothing left in her, she retched and heaved helplessly. Finally she staggered to the house and washed out her mouth, and washed her face and hands. She didn't look at herself in the mirror.

She put the rifle back and went out to the barn again, this time with a spade. She dug the grave big enough for them both, behind the barn where she could cover it with straw so that it wouldn't show. And when she was ready for them, she stopped. She would have to touch them after all. But the hair was just hair now, the silkiness and aliveness was gone. Just gray hair. She dragged them to the grave and covered them and hid the place with straw.

The children asked about the dogs, and she said they had run off just as mysteriously as they had come. Jeffrey said he was glad, they had been spooky. Juliette said she dreamed of them last night, and she was sorry they were gone. Annamarie didn't comment at all, but ran to the phone to call Jennifer.

Martin didn't believe her story. But he didn't question her. That night she told him. "I killed them."

A tremor passed over him. He nodded. "Are you all right?"

"I'm all right." she looked at him. "You're not surprised or shocked or disgusted? Something?"

"Not now. Maybe later. Now, nothing."

She nodded too. That was how she felt. They didn't talk about it again that night, but sat quietly, with the television off, neither of them reading or doing anything. They went to bed early and held each other hard until they fell asleep.

State of Grace

THE THINGS IN THE TREE were destroying my marriage. I think they were driving my husband crazy, but that is less easily demonstrated. I started a diary when I first saw them; after three entries I burned it. He would find it, I knew, and he would go out with nets and poles and catch them and sell them to a circus, or to a think tank for vivisection. He would find a way to profit.

This is all I know about them: they are small; their faces are as large as my fist; they are nut brown; they excrete their toxic wastes, if they have any, directly into the air. (Perhaps they are nuts that hatched the ultimate product. Perhaps all over the world walnuts are hatching walnut people; hazel nuts are hatching hazels; Brazil nuts are hatching wee brown Brazilians.) I don't think they ever come out of the tree. I stayed awake twenty-seven hours watching and none ever descended. I spread flour under the tree, pretending to Howard it was lime to sweeten the soil, and it was undisturbed for three days, until it rained. I wouldn't have used lime for fear of harming them if they did creep out during the darkest part of the night when my eyes were too heavy to stay open every single moment. The previous time, when I really did stay awake for twenty-seven hours, I never closed my eyes more than the normal time for blinking, and I drank nine cups of coffee during the last six hours. (I sneaked into the bushes when I had to, but I didn't close my eyes or go inside.)

Howard didn't want me to stay home and collect my unemployment. He was afraid his job as an airplane mechanic would vanish. He wants everyone to start flying again, to anywhere. Use credit if you don't have money. He thought the circles under my eyes were caused by financial worries, but I always leave worrying about money to him, because he's so good at it, and I often forget for days at a time.

He also thought that if I did stay home I should start having children. It was as good a time as any, he said, and even if he did get laid off, too, by the time the kid was born things would be back to normal again. What he really wished was that I would stay home and have his dinner ready every day and darn socks and spin and weave and churn butter and draw down an income too.

In the beginning I realized that he would make money with them, if he didn't decide they were parasites. He is more afraid of parasites than he is of other garden pests. He might have sprayed them with a biodegradable, not-harmful-to-warm-blooded-animals spray. The kind that has all sorts of precautions on the side in small print.

I began to worry about water for them and bought a birdbath. It cost twenty dollars and we fought about it. More marriages break up because of financial disputes than any other one thing, even sexual incompatibility. But people often lie to data gatherers, and this may not be true.

I got a birdbath without any paint in the bowl, and I had to shop all day for it, and used most of the gas in the tank. ($0.58 per gallon. He noticed, of course.) I scrubbed it thoroughly, even used steel wool, just in case there was something harmful in the finish. I have to scrub it every morning, because the birds enjoy it also, but I can't believe birds drink that much water in a day. It holds two gallons.

One day for a treat I'll put gingerale in it, or juice. They might like orange juice.

I began to worry about what they were finding to eat. There are green acorns on the tree, but they are very bitter. I tried one. That's when I got the bird feeder, and during the day I kept birdseed in it, but every night after dark I slipped out and put raisins and apples and carrot sticks on it for them. Sometimes they were gone the next day and sometimes they dried up, or the squirrels got them. Howard became suspicious of the feeder and he explained to me that birds don't feed at night. I caught him watching me later when I took out the supply of food. He was solicitous for several days. Then he made a joke of it, but soon after that he was watching me again, and, I fear, watching the tree.

The tree is in the center of our back yard, mature, dense, the perfect home for them, as long as no one suspects their presence. Our house is forty years old, with as much charm as a wet dishrag, but it was cheap, and the tree was there. An oak tree inspires confidence. I wonder if they watched the builders of our house, fearful that one day one of them would bring an ax. I think they are very brave to have stayed.

I worried about other things, too. What if a young one got scraped? I left out a box of Band-Aids. What if the squirrels were too aggressive? I bought a dart game and left the darts on the feeder. What if they really wanted to communicate and didn't have any way? I bought a tiny pad, the kind that has a three-inch pen attached by a chain.

When we had a barbecue, I tried to fan the smoke away from the tree.

They know I am their friend.

Howard brought home a dog, a great monster of a dog, with a foot-long, dripping tongue. The dog adores me, tolerates

Howard, and from day one he stared at the tree for long periods of time, not barking, not threatening, but aware. Howard knew something, but he couldn't believe what he knew.

"All right," Howard said, finally, holding my shoulder too hard. "What's in the tree?"

The dog growled, and Howard released me and stood with his hands on his hips. Howard's hips are too broad for a man. I told him he should ride a bicycle to work to trim off a couple of inches. He reached for me again and the monster dog ambled over.

"Acorns. Squirrels. Leaves. A nest of cardinals."

"You know damn well what I mean!"

Perhaps they are aliens, come to save the world. They are biding their time waiting for the eve of the final cataclysm before they act. Jung says most people who believe in flying saucers believe the aliens will save us.

Perhaps they are aliens, come to take over the world. They are biding their time, waiting for their forces to gather, to generate enough energy to make it a decisive victory when they act. The ones who don't believe the above tend to believe this.

A few think they would be passive, engaging in yet another spectator sport when the end comes.

I don't think they are aliens.

Howard thought they were monkeys, escaped from a zoo or a laboratory many years ago, that managed to survive in the wild. The wild of Fairdale, Kentucky, twenty minutes from the airport where Howard mechanics.

He didn't get as good a look as I did. It is my fault he glimpsed them at all, of course, so possibly I am not the tried and true friend to them that I would like to be.

Howard brought a camera for several hundred dollars. Airplane mechanics make very good money, more than many lawyers, especially those who work for the government. He took seven rolls of film, with thirty-six exposures on each roll. He had two hundred fifty-two pictures of oak leaves.

He took the ladder out to the tree and climbed it, but didn't stay long. All he saw was more leaves. I tried that, too, in the beginning. They are very clever at hiding. They have had thousands of years of practice. I am the first living person to have seen them clearly, and Howard, who glimpsed something that he prefers to call monkey, is the second, who almost did. We could have our names in the *Guinness Book of World Records*.

Howard called in exterminators. He didn't want them to kill anything, only identify the varmints in his tree.

The exterminators found the cardinal nest, and the squirrels, and they told us we have an infestation of southern oak moths. They produced three leaves with very small holes in them, which I am certain they made with their Bic pens. For fifty dollars they would spray the tree.

We were hardly speaking to each other. When he came home, the first thing he did was inspect the special shelf in the refrigerator where I kept things like Bing cherries, emperor grapes, Persian melons. Then he gulped down his dinner, holding his plate on his lap in order to turn around and keep the tree under observation. After dinner he sat on the patio and watched the tree until dark. Then he studied the pictures he had taken, using a magnifying glass, poring over each one for half an hour at least. By twelve he would stagger off to bed. He was looking haggard. He gave up bowling, and haircuts.

He thought they might migrate in the fall. He was getting desperate for fear they would leave one stormy night and his chance to make hundreds, even thousands of dollars would leave with them. One Saturday he went out and returned hours later with a tall, sunburned man who was the director of the zoo.

Howard took him to the tree and the man didn't even glance at the foliage, but began a minute examination of the ground,

taking almost an hour. He was looking for droppings, and there
are none. I visualized the tiny toilets, the complicated plumb-
ing, or else the nightly chamber pot ritual, the menial who must
empty and clean it in the gray dusk of dawn . . .

Howard was furious with the director. He shook him and
pointed upward. The man looked past him to where I was
standing on the patio and I tried to achieve a tortured smile, like
Joan Fontaine's. I shrugged just a little bit, sadly. Howard
whirled about and saw this, but of course the monster dog was
at my side, watching him very closely.

The zoo director left by the side gate while Howard stared at
me, his lips moving silently.

The next morning before I got up, Howard climbed the tree
again. I saw the ladder and waited, sipping coffee. He was up
a long time and when he came down he said nothing, didn't
even comment on the scratches on his hands, his cheeks, even
his ankles. I never knew an oak tree had stickers. I imagined a
tiny brown hand streaking out, a sharp dart raking, fast as
thought, withdrawing . . .

He tried to smoke them out in the afternoon, and the fire
marshal paid a call and explained the no-burn ordinance and
how much the fine would be if it happened again.

He bought Sominex and emptied it into the birdbath, and the
next morning there were two dopey squirrels draped over the
lowest branch of the tree, their tails inches away from the jaws
of the dog when it leaped, as it did over and over. The dog was
exhausted.

He bought sparkling burgundy. When I became giggly, he
begged me to tell him what was in the tree.

"A-corns and squir-rels, and a nest of car-din-als," I chanted
and giggled and hiccupped and, I think, fell asleep. It is possible
I said it more than once, because something made him angry
enough to sleep on the couch, and the next morning the phrase
was like a refrain in my head.

For over a week we didn't speak at all, not even a grunt, and the next week he muttered something about being sorry and it was the heat, and worry about his job, and maybe I should put in an application someplace or other. He heard that International Harvester was hiring secretarial help again. He wanted me to go to bed and I said I'd rather sleep with a crocodile. He slammed the door on his way out.

He came back with a string of perfectly awful beads, all iridescent and shiny and it is impossible to tell what they are even supposed to be. One of us forgave the other and I made him promise to leave *them* alone and triumphantly he disclosed that he had had a tape recorder going all the time and now he had proof that I knew something was in our oak tree and there was no point in my pretending he was crazy. I am certain he is a secret Nixon Republican.

I said soothingly that of course something lived in the oak tree and its children lived under the lilac bush and its relatives lived in the honeysuckle and everyone knew all about them. He tried to hit me, and the monster dog was outside guarding the tree, so I had to fend him off myself, and eventually we did go to bed, just as we both had planned from the start. After he was sleeping I got up and erased the tape.

It became open warfare. Neither of us was willing to sleep while the other was awake. He began to eat the Bing cherries. We both looked haggard.

Someone at work told him about infrared film and he planned to spend the night taking pictures, after the air cooled so *they* would show up better. At dusk I climbed the tree and moved about here and there, but eventually I had to climb back down, for fear I might fall asleep and fall out. He was snoring. I finished the roll of film, taking a dozen pictures of the monster dog, who was dreaming of the Great Chase in the Sky. He was smiling, his legs twitching, his impossible tongue now and then snaking out to wipe his chops.

It would take several weeks to have the film developed. No

one does it locally. Several weeks was too long. Already, in September, the evenings were cool, and if there was an early frost, it could drive them to their southern homes. He was positive they would migrate.

He bought a cat. It refused to climb the tree even though he put it on the trunk where it clung and looked at him hissing. It turned and sprang to the ground and he caught it and put it back, higher. The monster dog was tied to the water spigot, straining to get free, making weird tortured-dog noises. The cat twisted and jumped and jumped again, nearly halfway across the yard; the dog broke loose, and they both leaped over the fence and vanished, the dog baying like the Baskerville hound. Howard had to go after them before someone shot the dog. When they got back, the dog's feet were sore and it came to me, grinning, its tongue dripping like a hose, expecting high praise for its heroism. Howard didn't speak. The cat never came back.

He was plotting. He was having a steak and beer party in the back yard, inviting all his bowling buddies and a few extra men who were going to help him cut down the old rotten tree, net the possums—possums?—and then feast.

"Someone will get killed," I pointed out. "The tree is over eighty feet tall." He smiled his smuggest smile and I threw my cup at him. He ducked and dialed another number.

The next day I bought clothesline and pulleys and made them an escape route to a maple tree at the property line. I fastened a small Easter basket to the rope and if they were as clever as I thought, they would figure out the pulley arrangement. If not, they could get out hand over hand. I explained to them what they had to do, and then, to be certain they understood, I wrote it down for them and left the message in the basket. I was still worried that they wouldn't know how to use the basket, and at three in the morning, I took out the awful beads Howard had brought home and put them in the basket and for half an hour worked it back and forth. They were watching. They watch everything; that is their strength.

Howard brought home the steaks. (Two dollars ninety-eight cents a pound, twelve of them, all more than 2 pounds. I could have cried.) There was a case of beer in a cooler on the patio. I fed steaks to the dog, but even the monster couldn't eat more than three of them. Howard bought replacements and stood by the refrigerator every time I moved.

He carried the chain saw about with him, afraid I would hex it.

"Get lost!" Howard said Saturday morning. "We're going to cut that damn tree down, catch those things and cage them and then eat steak and drink beer and play poker. Bug off!"

"We're being childish," I said. "I was bored and played a game, pretended I saw something, and you convinced yourself that you saw it too. That's what children do. I'll go look for a job Monday. No more games."

He made a noncommittal noise.

"Or maybe I'm pregnant. Sometimes pregnant women imagine strange things, instead of craving strange foods."

He glared at me.

The men began to gather and there was a lot of consultation about the tree, with several of them walking around it thoughtfully, spilling beer as they gestured. As if they knew something about cutting down trees. They would get drunk and he would cut someone's head off, I thought.

I watched him start the saw and winced at the noise. I didn't know if *they* had escaped or not; there was no way to tell. Someone pointed upward and Howard stopped the saw and again they all considered the task. It had been pointed out that in movies they always cut off branches and the top first. Otherwise the tree would surely demolish the house when it fell.

Someone got the ladder and Howard climbed it and started the saw again. He brought it down to the tree limb, hesitated, turned off the saw, dropped it to the ground and climbed back down.

He was trembling. "I just wanted to give the old lady a scare. Show her who's boss. Let's eat." He didn't look at me.

He got drunk and after the others had gone he told me the saw had come alive, turned on him. He had seen his leg being cut off, had seen it falling and had thought it was beautiful that way. The saw was turning in his hands when he switched it off and dropped it.

I should have had more faith in their ability to protect themselves.

I don't believe it was his leg.

Howard has forgotten about them, pretends he never believed in them in the first place. He never glances at the tree, and he burned all the pictures he took, even the infrared ones.

I have too much to do to work outside the house any more. He accepts that. I am charting all their likes and dislikes. When I left them chopped turnip, there was a grease fire that could have burned down the house. I crossed off turnips. When I find out-of-season fruits, like mangoes, cut up just so with a touch of lemon juice, something nice happens, like the telegram from my mother on my birthday. They like for me to wear soft, flowing, white gowns. My blue jeans brought a thunderstorm, and lightning hit the pole out front and we were without electricity for twenty-four hours.

There is a ritual I go through now when Howard wants to go to bed with me. He doesn't object. It excites him, actually, to see me undress under the tree.

They liked the mouse I caught for them, and I'm wondering if they would like a chick, or a game hen. The mouse got Howard a Christmas bonus. I know a place that sells live chicks. . . .

REMEMBER IT DOESN'T GROW ON TREES

ENERGY CONSERVATION -
IT'S YOUR CHANCE TO SAVE, AMERICA

Department of Energy, Washington, D.C.